ABOUT THE AUTHOR

Syd Moore was a lecturer and a presenter on *Pulp*, the Channel 4 books programme, before becoming a writer. She is the author of the mystery novels *The Drowning Pool* and *Witch Hunt*. *The Twelve Strange Days of Christmas* is part of the Essex Witch Museum series, which includes *Strange Magic, Strange Sight, Strange Fascination* and *Strange Tombs*. She lives in Essex, where her novels are set.

THE TWELVE
STRANGE DAYS OF
CHRISTMAS

SYD MOORE

A Point Blank Book

First published by Point Blank, an imprint of Oneworld Publications, 2019
Some of these stories were first published in the ebook *The Strange Casebook*, 2018
Reprinted, 2020

ISBN 978-1-78607-680-9
ISBN 978-1-78607-681-6 (ebook)

Printed and bound in Great Britain by Clays Ltd, Elcograf S.p.A.

Oneworld Publications
10 Bloomsbury Street
London WC1B 3SR
England

Stay up to date with the latest books,
special offers, and exclusive content from
Oneworld with our newsletter

Sign up on our website
oneworld-publications.com

CONTENTS

[definition] Strange /streɪn(d)ʒ/

Adjective: strange
1.   Unusual or surprising; difficult to understand or explain.

Comparative adjective: stranger; *superlative adjective:* strangest

Synonyms: Odd, curious, peculiar, funny, bizarre, weird, uncanny, queer, unexpected, unfamiliar, abnormal, atypical, anomalous, different, out of the ordinary, out of the way, extraordinary, remarkable, puzzling, mystifying, mysterious, perplexing, baffling, unaccountable, inexplicable, incongruous, uncommon, irregular, singular, deviant, aberrant, freak, freakish, surreal, alien.

SEPTIMUS AND THE SHAMAN

'Thank you, dear Samuel,' said the old man as he took the glass of brandy. With customary reverence, he held it up to examine against the light of the fire roaring in the fireplace and smiled as something within it kindled a memory.

The young man, Sam, took his own liberal serving to the armchair opposite and peered over the top of the tumbler. His respect and affection for Septimus Strange was great. Often he found himself surprised by the old curator's generosity of spirit. Many times he was impressed by his esoteric knowledge that was both extraordinarily expansive, some might even say supernaturally so, and also ever-expanding. Even in his ninth decade Septimus Strange displayed an intense curiosity about the world that had never been sated, nor gave any signs of becoming less urgent. His mind was energetic and appreciative and in conversation displayed a sprightly energy that bubbled and sparked away inside.

Perhaps that was why Sam had been rather taken aback when the old man's mood had appeared to dampen and fall as they had left the conference they had been attending and made the long journey back to the Witch Museum.

He had grown thoughtful and reflective rather than chirpy and excited as was his usual manner after engaging in lively discussion with like-minded professionals.

'I thought you might have enjoyed this afternoon's session rather more than you did, Septimus,' Sam ventured after the pair of them had consumed a good centimetre of the brandy liqueur.

The old man lifted his head. His lips had thinned over the years and, this evening, his shoulders were definitely too narrow for the suit he was wearing. He looked to Sam with distracted amusement and a smile that became full. 'Enjoy it? Oh I did, dear boy, I did.'

'What was it then?' asked Sam. 'I felt that you lost some of your customary effervescence, for which you are so renowned. It was when they produced that Icelandic headdress, wasn't it? I saw a shadow pass over you.' He paused and, to be clear, added, 'Metaphorically speaking.'

'Oh yes. Then? Did you? The artefact, I suppose, took me back a bit. Reminded me of something I was once told. A prediction of sorts.'

'Did that upset you?'

Septimus frowned. 'It made me think a little too long.'

'Well,' said Sam as he swirled his glass and smelled the thick, sweet fumes of the spirit, 'I couldn't have concentrated on anything else. I was completely blown away by the stitching of the leather, those runic symbols. Wonderful to touch something like that.'

Septimus did not react for a moment, so Sam continued. He had been enthralled with the artefact and wanted to voice the feeling and learn what his mentor thought. 'Those teeth strung round the feathers. The crafting of the mask itself . . . Personally, I thought it was,' he took a breath, 'magnificent.'

Septimus turned in his chair to face Sam more directly. 'Oh no. I agree with you, Sam, indeed I do. I would say it was an excellent piece, in fact. Did you see the looks and expressions of reverence on the faces of the other curators? They were rapt, so attentive and careful as they held the headdress like so.' He rested his glass on the arm of his chair and held up the imaginary artefact. '"Ohhhhhhhh, how different it is", "aaaahh – the majesty", and so on.' He put down the invisible headdress on his lap and fetched back the brandy. 'And yet. I wonder if such a thing had been found on British soil – would it have been treated with such awe and respect? Such veneration by academics? I think it would more likely be relegated to "folk history" and not worthy of much regard.'

Sam had heard sentiment like this before. 'But we recognise that familiarity breeds contempt,' he said at last. 'And you know as well as I do, Sept, that our moon talismans, hag stones, and athames have generated as much admiration in Scandinavia as their headdresses and artefacts do here.'

The old man brought his head down to his chest as if chastised, then looked up suddenly. 'Quite right, Sam. This is why I need you. Why your appearance in my life has been so thoroughly,' he paused and sniffed the air, 'symbiotic,' he said, pleased his brain had supplied the correct adjective. 'You keep me on the right path. That is, not the left. Nor the right.' Then he winked. 'Sometimes when one reaches my age, it is all too easy for one's gaze, one's thoughts, to fall on what is not well with the world, rather than appreciate in it all that is true and fair.'

Sam laughed and nodded, feeling rather pleased. 'Surely not,' he said. 'Though I understand what you mean.'

'I know you do, dear Sam,' the old man agreed.

The silence that unfurled between them was not awkward or discomforting, but quite the opposite. The pair enjoyed it and refilled their glasses.

After a while Septimus looked into the fire and said, 'Did I ever tell you about my encounter with an Icelandic shaman?'

The young man's attention was brought swiftly to brook. 'No, you did not! And now you cannot keep it to yourself.'

It was Septimus's turn to rattle out a laugh. 'Oh, it was many, many years ago,' he said, and started, as the fire in the hearth spluttered and gave out a spark, which thankfully landed on the tiles and not the carpet. 'I haven't said your name yet,' Septimus whispered to it.

Sam frowned: that was odd. He wasn't sure whether to challenge the old man on it or to let it go. Was it a sign, he wondered? Septimus was getting on a bit after all. But before he could act on any impulse the owner of the Witch Museum withdrew his gaze and said, 'I had received an assignment in Reykjavik. It was during the war. We had invaded Iceland then, you know.'

Sam met his friend's gaze with brows hoisted high.

'Oh yes, that was a thing,' Septimus said, misjudging Sam's countenance.

'I have a vague notion that that happened,' said Sam, deciding the aside to the fire was an uncharacteristic expression of whimsy, most likely brought about by the warmth and the brandy. He dismissed his initial misgivings and took up the conversation again. 'We invaded Iceland?'

Septimus nodded. 'It was a strategic island. Important for the North Atlantic sea lanes. And very well laid out for naval bases and air bases and so on. Not many people seem to be aware of what the Brits did back then, but anyhow, I digress. As I said, I was instructed by Commander Fleet back at the bureau, to investigate a manifesting medium on tour in Reykjavik. The authorities at the time were alarmed by the man's accuracy, although this particular fellow was rather a harbinger of doom, predicting, amongst other things, sea strikes and sinkings, great losses of life. Fleet himself was wondering where the precision came from, if we might be able to use it somehow. Certainly, he was of the idea that the chap's latest warnings necessitated some tight investigation. So I was despatched by plane.

'Reykjavik is a small city. When I arrived, I located my lodgings with ease. I was to board with a pleasant landlady and another British captain. Once oriented and settled, I learned that the celebrated clairvoyant was performing that very night. So I started work straight away.

'I must tell you that I arrived at the theatre with an open mind. The medium seemed neat and well presented, though he had a stuttering delivery, which did not impress me. He also appeared to have some irritating manners, often putting his hand to his mouth and coughing. Yet every human being has their own manner of dealing with stage nerves. Or perhaps, I thought, he was suffering with a cold. I took notes as he went through the usual manifestation techniques.' Septimus looked at Sam and winced. 'Cheesecloth was produced, I'm pretty sure. Regurgitated from here.' He tapped his tummy. 'I could smell stomach acids. The lights in the auditorium had been subdued and there was some kind of fluorescence in the cloth that gave off a ghastly glow. Of course, the manifestation was supposed to be the spirit of one ancient guildsman of Reykjavik who had returned to warn the population of fresh impending disaster, which again I recorded. The prediction was vague, involving water and lead. Nothing that could be pinned down, but I'm sure the theatrics helped convince a proportion of those in attendance that they were in the presence of a skilled necromancer. After the "channelling" of his phantom guide, the medium addressed several members of the audience, attesting that he was receiving messages from various departed friends and family who had passed over to the spirit world. He did appear to score high, with some accuracy on at least sixty per cent of his attempts, which was rather more than I was used to seeing. The audience lapped this up with cries of astonishment and sometimes tears. I found that the clairvoyant was sympathetic and kind to those with whom he spoke and I did, at one point, wonder if there was really any harm in any of it. But then remembered my mission and, as the evening panned out, it became clear to me that the man had *a relationship* with the venue holders. Reykjavik was not as densely populated as many of our British cities. The organisers were local people who appeared

6

to be acquainted with many of their audience members. I have no doubt that, because there was a ticket price and a profit to be made, both parties – owners and performer – were to benefit from an exchange of information. Towards the end, as some kind of finale, the medium was able to elicit very positive responses from one of the members who broke down and wept at the message from his late brother. Uncanny accuracy was contained in the messages addressed to him. I later discovered from the woman sitting next to me that he lived next door to the venue's owners.'

'Usually the way,' said Sam.

Septimus nodded. 'But that is not the matter. The matter comes later. When the performance ended, I took my hat and coat and made to get out before the rush of the audience. As I left the theatre I found a woman waiting for me in the shadows. She did not speak but handed me a card.'

Sam shifted himself up in his seat. 'Oh yes?'

'On that card was written – "Not all in Iceland is false. If you wish to see truth meet me at eight o'clock tomorrow night. Come alone."'

'Intriguing,' said Sam and looked at the old man closely. His vigour was returning – the fire in the hearth jumped about his eyes as he returned to his memory.

'Indeed.'

'Of course you went?'

'I did. But it was not an immediate resolution. One must be careful how one treads in an occupied territory.'

Septimus noted the rise of his younger friend's eye and explained. 'It could have been a trap.'

'Ah yes, of course.'

'And I had leads to follow up with regard to the neighbour.'

'Quite.'

'But at eight o'clock the following night I was to be found outside the theatre in the darkened streets of Reykjavik.'

Sam looked on, committing the details to memory. He had a feeling things were about to get even more interesting.

'It's funny,' said Septimus to his brandy glass. 'My memory of the consequent incident is as clear as a bell, but for the life of me I can barely recall what the woman who met me looked like. It's almost as if her face was slippery. I can only see a blur and have a sense that, although she was certainly far from good-looking, she was not exactly ugly.'

Sam supressed a smile at the loose frankness of his older friend. Despite Septimus's elastic soul, his tolerance and empathy for the human species, at times the years between them betrayed contrasting attitudes shaded by different upbringings.

'It may have had something to do with the contents of the peace pipe I smoked,' Septimus speculated.

Again, Sam started. The old man was always surprising him.

Septimus continued. 'There was most certainly an amount of hallucinogen, a mind-altering compound, in there. Fly agaric most likely. Sami shamans often used them as a trigger in their cross-dimensional journeys.' He saw Sam frown and added a pacifier. 'Rituals.' Then in an undertone he cast his eyes to the walls of the museum and, as if he were speaking to some invisible presence within them, muttered, 'The boy has

8

a keen mind, but there are some ideas he's not yet prepped for. The time will come of course. Never fear.'

Sam could not conceal fresh concern at the deviant tangent that their conversation had just sprung. Depression ballooned in his stomach. He hoped to God that the old boy's asides to the walls and hearth were no indication of brain decay.

'But I get ahead of myself,' said Septimus. Almost as if he had heard Sam's thoughts, his words became sharper, well-enunciated, focused. 'The woman – I have in my mind that her name was Hekla, though I am not entirely sure. But let us call her Hekla, to ease the telling of the tale. Her real name is not important. Hekla was of average beauty though heavy-browed. She spoke little as we drove out of Reykjavik into the flat rocky scrubs of the island. As we approached our destination, she turned off the headlights and slowed the car to a crawl.

'Out the windows I could see a mountain rising on the horizon. I expected us to take one of the forks in the roads that veered round to circle the base. And yet, that is not the path we followed. We took the road that led towards the coast, but soon turned off onto a mud track. I could feel from the bumps and lurches that there was no smoothness underneath the wheels. This was a track little travelled. And, I must confide, Sam my boy, I did wonder if I had been unwise to keep this excursion to myself. I had left no word with my landlady, nor the captain, of where I might be found, so should I come to grief, no one would know. See, I had not yet met my wife at this point, and, as a bachelor with no dependants, I was accustomed to taking care of no one but myself. And, although I was no youth, my heart was packed tight with ideas of valour, noble discovery, and the certain integrity of intuition.'

In his chair Sam nodded. He knew what Septimus meant, though trust in his own intuition was not something he had yet mastered.

'So,' Septimus continued. 'Second thoughts. Presently Hekla stopped the car. I could not see why we might have come here to the base of the little mountain. We got out. Hekla pointed upwards to the summit and made off. Again, I wondered if this was the right course of action, but with little else to do and no access to Hekla's car keys, I was faced with no other choice. I followed her and we began our ascent.

'As we scaled the dusty boulders that lined the sides, I humorously voiced the opinion that if I had known we were to be rock climbing I would not have worn my best brogues. Hekla apologised but reassured me that my sartorial sacrifice would be worth what I was to find when we reached our final destination.

'It was an exerting climb. About halfway up, Hekla began to move sideways, her hands gripping onto the rocks that protruded from the cliff. As I scrambled after her, I saw that the rear side of the mountain, hidden from the road, had fallen away, leaving something of a hollow there.

'The rocks, at this point, became smaller and less fixed and we had to slow down to ensure we didn't lose our footing. Gradually I realised this was not a mountain we were making our way across, but a volcano. Extinct, I hoped, or certainly dormant. Though the air was cold, crisping our breath, the rocks underneath our hands were not.

'Hekla pointed down to the crater. I could see pricks of light flickering there. We descended, stumbling over black rocks and boulders, and as we grew closer, I saw that they were little bonfires. It did not become clear until we had reached the bottom of the crater, a kind of plateau, that they were arranged to form a circle. A circle that was pierced by a dark, murky crack. As soon as I saw it, I had the impulse to run to its dark yawn, to crouch down and reassure myself there was no dancing red larva beneath it, but Hekla steered me away to a shelter fashioned from canvas and draped with moss and furs. The trappings must have had the effect of camouflaging it for I had not seen it on our descent.

'She rustled the flap and told me to wait, then disappeared inside.

'I was happy to study my surroundings. There was much to take in about this place Hekla had brought me to: the craggy lip of the crater in silhouette against the luminous galactic dust of the Milky Way. The primal hardness of the black rocks – larva spat once from the earth's core and then hardened into solidity by Old Man Time – these black rocks, under the moonshine, took on a lunar cast. I had never been anywhere like it before. It was,' he paused and let his smile float skywards, '. . . it was marvellous.'

Sam discerned that his friend was moved and tried hard to peer into his world and imagine what he was describing.

'It is possible, of course,' Septimus continued, 'that the imposing surroundings had altered my state of consciousness.

Elevated it. And that perhaps the darkness, the sensory deprivation, had caused other senses to overcompensate. For sure, I cannot say. But soon I was roused from my deep contemplation by Hekla who bade me enter the shelter.

'Inside, it seemed more cave than tepee. Full of smoke and odours of herbs. There was another fire burning in a stone hearth at its centre. Sitting around it, several natives were chanting and singing in low, softened voices, some old song. I was obliged to disrobe and don something that resembled more of a leather cloak. It was fur-lined and warm, which was a relief, as although I had not removed my trousers and vest, Hekla had insisted on taking my coat, jacket and shirt. Outside it was not warm.

'I was moved to a vacant space in the circle and instructed to sit down, then, as the chanting increased, a peace-pipe was passed around. I did not smoke at the time, but felt that to refuse such an offering would constitute bad manners, and for sure I was not only a stranger in their midst, but also an uninvited British invader. I accepted the pipe with respect and, much to the amusement of the natives gathered there, managed to take down a few spluttering lungfuls before it was passed on.

'By and by, I noted a change in my perceptions. The colours in the tent grew more intense. I became impressed by a sense of drama, as if we were all gathered to await a special guest. I had the notion that I was not in the company of human beings but visiting guardians of some ancient earth secret, who had, in a moment of extreme benevolence, allowed me access. I could not see Hekla but I was filled with a sense of gratitude for her note, for bringing me to witness, to experience, this most sacred of rites.

'Then suddenly the chanting stopped. Everyone got to their feet. I was pulled up then led out of the tent and round into the circle of fires.

'There, in the middle, was another fire I had not seen before and which had only just been lit. Behind it, cross-legged, sat an old, old man, who had not been in the tent. He was dressed in shaman's robes, feathers had been plaited into his hair and his face was decorated with paint. I think he was not native but may have come from Finland. Perhaps one of the Sami. A travelling shaman. Displaced from his land. Many were.' Septimus looked into his brandy as the fire danced through it. 'I was taken to him and presented. As I bowed, an understanding seemed to pass over his eyes and he invited me to take a place opposite him, the other side of his fire.

'Of course, I accepted and sat down watching the tiny flames lick at the wood and coal. Above them the air warped and through the sparks and smoke that rose, I was drawn to the shaman's dark eyes. They appeared to me, in that state, full of infinite wisdom. The wise man's leathery skin, was tight and fast and tanned over eons by exposure to and intercourse with the natural world. And again, I had the impression of vast arcane knowledge and, paradoxically you might think, an idea of great sophistication. It was humbling. I felt gauche within myself. I think the shaman realised these feelings of mine for he directed one of the women to bring me a drum.

'When I took it into my arms, I felt a pang of excitement and an exquisite tremble of belonging.

'There were ten in the outer circle now, positioned between the bonfires. My eyes had adjusted: I could see that they came from different places. A couple were blonde, classically Nordic, others were graced with olive skin, more yet were pale-eyed and red-haired. At a signal given by the shaman, they all instantly began to move as one and together in a unity of motion started to beat their drums. Slow at first. Bang, bang, bang.' Septimus held the palm of his hand rigid and struck his lap. 'Like so. A tight, short sound. Powerful.

'The shaman spoke to me, some words in a language I did not understand, but I had the idea he was instructing me to copy his rhythm, which was slightly faster than the rest. So I moved my hands to the skin and began to beat it. By increments the rhythm sped up. Now, along with the shaman, there were twelve of us there in that circle drumming. All of us joined in a synchronous beating out of a most hallowed rhythm.'

'What was the drum like?' Sam asked, unable to stopper his mouth. He was curious as to the ritual that his friend was describing and craved more detail.

'Yes,' said Septimus. 'You've got it. It was a Noaidi rune drum. A replica of which we have downstairs in the international section. Very good. Well spotted, Samuel. Commander Fleet had the likeness made when I recounted the incident. He later gave me the copy, after he had acquired an original himself. The drum I beat was fashioned from wood and, I think, calf skin. A number of symbols had been painted across the membrane – a sun, a man with antlers, lines representing people, animals, landscapes, spirits and gods. They were not unlike some of the hieroglyphs to be found on Doctor John Dee's disc, although those represented Dee's language of the angels and the symbology of the rune drum signifies meaning of another kind.'

Sam nodded, curiosity sated, and Septimus returned to his tale. 'The shaman beat the drum. As I said, the rhythm was old, captivating, like the sound of heartbeats, the pulse of life. I could see the shaman's eyes closing, that he was going into a trance and at the same time I too could feel myself following. I continued to drum, my body seeming to operate by itself, almost on autopilot. The fire began to crackle and roar as the shaman recited words, intoning them like a Latin verse. I felt my spirit grow sharp, and just then as I breathed in it seemed that time slowed.

'The moment lengthened.

'Everything stilled.

'The universe swirled and eased its constant motion.

'I was conscious of sitting under the umbrella of night and felt the gaze of the moon on my cheeks, the firmness of the earth beneath me, the vibration of its low heartbeat thrumming through me. My ears detected a soft murmur, as if the unseen world was stirring and becoming visible. I became aware of everything living around me. Life, you see, life.'

Septimus cleared his throat, an unconscious action which betrayed the physical changes in his body that the remembrance had brought about. 'And these sensations,' he went on, his voice trembling, 'they clashed and joined together, a confluence. As one, even stronger than they had been before. A united force. And I felt this *force* reach into the very fabric of my living being and twist and pluck out a thread of a feeling, an impulse so often buried in modern man. But a sensitivity that is there, that still exists, that continues despite the onslaught of technological progress, despite the clamour of the modern world, despite the de-sensitisation, the layering of logic and social mores and expectation. And this sensitivity, this *untwisted* response, my dear friend, came to the fore. It made me acknowledge my place, my identity in the vastness of the cosmos, and understand the great force, the immensity and wonder of existence.'

Sam watched the old man's features shine, as if animated by a burning sun within.

'It is a thing to feel it,' he said, shaking his head. Though he was not sad: on his lips played a smile. 'And if one feels it and does not suppress it, then one cannot prevent oneself from opening further. And if one is thus open, then a two-way exchange may begin. So brief, so wondrous, so rare. "Wordless, notion-less communication with the universe" is what I later scribbled in my notes.'

He sat back and tapped his glass. Sam wondered if he was going to give up his narration and instead take his mind back to that moment and enclose himself within its richness once more.

He wouldn't have blamed him. The mere description, he was aware, had unleashed a response inside his own self. And, as he sat by the fire in Septimus's lounge, he became aware of a feeling at the back of his head, an itch or a notion or perhaps an 'understanding', that some of the exhibits beneath him in the Witch Museum might be moving, vibrating, responding to the energy being created here like a séance, singing to him in a silent, collective voice, a hymn.

'I gave into the feeling,' Septimus said at length. 'I closed my eyes and yet continued to be sentient of everything around me – the movement of the stars above, at particle level – turning, spinning, the swirl of a mote of dust in the horsehead nebula, dancing, pulsing. And I could *feel* everything too. As I breathed in I detected the temperature of the air that pushed into my lungs and sank through the membranes into my blood, oxygenating it.

'And as I was caught in that long deliberate moment, I heard the shaman call out. The words were indistinct, blurred. Something like "Aka" or "Akka" or "Barka".

'The sound prompted me to open my eyes. As I did, the drumming stopped. Time slowed to a point, then froze. Everyone in the circle, cross-legged and sweating, paused in their banging of the drums, hands held high, as still as statues. The stars ceased their blinking. The earth stopped its spinning.

'I became aware of a spray of red liquid emerging slowly from the crevice beside us. I could not move my head to it for I too was frozen in the moment. But the liquid, I saw out of the corner of my eye, dazzling gold, bubbling red, billowed in mid-air, and swirled into a foamy form. It was not party to the laws of time or gravity or anything else as shallow and base. Though I could not see it with clarity I knew, if I were

17

to look, the most ferocious set of features would stare back at me. And so I tried not to meet its gaze, but to lower my eyes in supplication to this fiery dragon-like creature, fashioned from larva and flame.

'I fastened my eyes on the shaman, whom I could see moving fractionally, his hair, trapped in the lengthening of time, quivered languidly as it responded to the fluctuation of his hands on the drum.

'And then I saw behind him another man standing. Another shaman, identical in every way to the one sitting across the fire from me, though incandescent, transparent. He took a step forward and passed through the solid form of the shaman on the ground, and I knew suddenly that I was seeing the wise man's spirit body.

'As clear as I see you now,' said Septimus. 'And it – he – turned and gestured to the unfurling matter that was tossing and rearing from the crack in the ground.

'In the next minute, I heard his voice in my head. "The spirit of the fire has words for you," he said. "A warning."

'There was little else I could do but wait for what was to come.

'There was more movement by the crack, then I heard the words, "He, who you see, is not what he be. The mark of your foe is upon him." And immediately I was caught by an image of the man I had inspected the night before. My mind had summoned it so clearly that I had the sense that I was not there, right then, within the mountainside crater, but had been drawn away through the air, to float about the form of the clairvoyant on stage at the theatre. And I experienced the very strange feeling that I was levitating around him unseen, listening to the squeak of his skin as pinpricks of sweat transcended through his pores. I peered into his eyes and saw the black fibres of his irises dilate and expand with fear. I felt the motion of the air as his hand disturbed it, flying to cover his mouth as his tongue spasmed and crinked to adopt a lisp and cover the Germanic consonants creeping into his speech. And, of course, it came to me right then that indeed he was a spy. And as soon as that recognition flared, the image disappeared. The air tensed and flexed. Time popped and burst. The fire between myself and the shaman blazed up, the drummers recommenced their noisy banging, the shaman's hair moved again.

'I blinked hard, and when I next opened my eyes, the shaman was shaking me. The fire was long since gone. Only ashes and cinders. Around us was darkness and silence. We were alone but for Hekla.

'I was disoriented and began to collect myself. The shaman was saying something insistent. He had thrown rune stones on the earth and was pointing to one. I tried to focus but my vision was still rather odd, certainly blurred.

'He repeated his words. This time I could not understand his meaning. It was Hekla who translated: "There are more warnings." She pointed to a stone which I now began to see was carved with a particular forking runic symbol. "You must take care of your women. They will die in violence," Hekla told me.'

In his chair Sam gasped and shivered. For once, he didn't know what to say.

'"But," she pointed to a rune, "there will be one, who will come." The shaman spoke to her in a low voice. "Synthesis," she translated. "One will come who will show. She will come. She will go."'

Septimus checked Sam. 'I wasn't sure what he meant then of course. But I knew it frightened me. All of it. And in fact, I believe the shock of what he said, combined with the lack of heat contrived to bring about something of a fainting fit. For I remember struggling to my feet and then nothing more.'

'Nothing at all?' asked Sam.

'When I came round, I was wrapped in blankets in the back of Hekla's car. I had a headache and a dry mouth and felt like I had gone two rounds in the ring with Raging Bull. When we reached my lodgings, Hekla conversed with my landlady and I was put straight to bed and nursed over the next two days with lots of meat broth.'

'Oh,' said Sam. 'And that was that?'

'Well, not quite. When I had fully recovered, I organised a secure line with the commander. At my request the alleged medium was taken into custody and interrogated. He did not have enough stamina to resist for long and, sure enough, as my vision revealed, he later confessed to being a German plant.'

'Interesting,' said Sam and ruminated over the implications. 'And what say you of that? Your vision?'

'There are two or three possibilities, but I prefer the idea that the amplification of my senses resulted in my concentration fastening on a point and inspecting it more closely than I had done before. The medium was, after all, the reason I had been sent there in the first place.'

Sam looked down as he asked, 'And what of the, er, prophecies?'

'Dear boy, my daughter, it is true, died in a tragic and awful manner, but no one knows what became of my wife. I wondered . . .' but he did not complete his sentence.

Though eager to hear what the old man wondered, Sam was not going to press him now. He watched Septimus's forehead writhe with creases as he wrestled with dark emotions. Losing a daughter in an accident was awful, the worst. A wife disappearing into thin air, well, it was not worth thinking about. Sam couldn't imagine the anguish his friend had experienced and was suddenly possessed by the urge to wrest him from the contemplation of his life's appalling tragedies. 'I see,' he said to move Septimus on. 'But what of the demons – the fire spirit that you saw?'

His colleague's face came up. 'Now of that I'm not sure. There is a common understanding amongst those who dabble in such things that if one is able to discover the true name of a demon or elemental or such, then one is empowered to call it up and draw upon its energy.'

'So you think there is something in it?' Sam pressed on, considering whether Septimus might offer up a crystal of truth, a reason that he could hold up to his own internal light and marvel at. 'Do you actually think there was?'

'It is an experience that has stayed with me, over the years, for sure.'

'Then we should write it up. Display your story beside the Noaidi drum.'

In his chair, Septimus chuckled. 'I don't think so, dear boy.'

'No? Why not? Ah, military secrets.'

Septimus straightened his back and leaned towards his friend. 'Secrets indeed!' And much to Sam's surprise, he gave a little laugh. 'I'll say to you what Commander Fleet advised me.'

'Yes? What's that?' Sam leaned in, all ears, waiting for pearls of wisdom to fall.

'I'd keep quiet on this one, Strange, if I were you. Don't want the world knowing you were stoned. I'd hazard it was the drugs.'

'The drugs?' said Sam, hugely disappointed.

'That's right,' Septimus nodded but there was a glimmer in his eyes.

'And do you think that?' Sam persisted. 'That it was the drugs?'

But Septimus just smiled and finished his drink. 'My dear, that would be telling. There are some things you have to find out for yourself. Or else what's the point of the journey?'

SNOWY

This was the third white Christmas that Norah had spent alone in Adder's Fork. Well, not alone. Just without the company of fellow homo sapiens. Not that she minded. Her home was warm, and she was well-loved and well cared for by her family of doting felines.

Her own clan of humans had died off years since.

Sort of.

She had a nephew, Colin, somewhere in Florida, who wrote to her twice a year – once on her birthday and once at Christmas. But they were boastful letters packed with photos of broad, rosy children, who got fatter by the year and infinitely less interesting. She was convinced Colin paid her his dues to ensure his stake in any bequest she might leave when she finally waltzed off this mortal coil. Although she had no plans to just yet.

Norah was quite comfortable in the two parts of the house that she tended to frequent these days: the kitchen and sitting room, with infrequent visits to the cloakroom across the hall. She had given up bathing and the cats didn't mind, so she only used the bathroom for essential ablutions when absolutely required. A chamber pot under the bed was a useful aid in this regard.

Putting aside the remains of the microwaved Christmas pud, she shuffled to her favourite seat: the high-back armchair, next to the Calor gas heater. It had a view out of the French windows onto the long lawn, the summerhouse and, beyond that, the orchard with the pear tree, plums and cobnuts. It was a splendid view that she had enjoyed for decades. At first with her husband, David, then, after him, with a succession of feline friends and acquaintances.

Her first was Sooty. A rather unoriginal name it was true, but she had never anticipated having a pet. Not least a cat. She had thought them rather cruel beasts, aloof and haughty and cold. Too independent by far and fickle with their affections. Much, she thought, like herself. Perhaps that is why she had let Sooty into her heart so quickly – so much of the cat's nature seemed to mirror her own. In the end she had been, it was true to say, utterly overwhelmed by the cat's persistence, his gifts of a partridge, several mice and a vole. Finally, she found that she was flattered by the fact the creature had chosen *her*.

For who was she?

Norah Davenport was just a little widow, old, with as wrinkled dugs as Tiresias and baggy at the seams like another cat that had delighted children a long time ago. Not someone any right-minded feline might court for company. But then, she had begun to realise, these cats weren't just your run-of-the-mill furry friends.

These cats were discerning.

These cats were hers.

It had taken a few months to work Sooty out, but eventually it was Mozart that had given Norah the clue. *The Marriage of Figaro* to be precise. For it had been her sister's favourite. Black-haired, dark-eyed Lydia had always loved it so.

It was on the anniversary of Lydia's birthday that the penny finally dropped.

In the evening Norah had got out the 78 to honour her sister, in a fashion. She had fixed herself a G and T, settled into her chair, and not noticed the cat staring in rapture at the old gramophone. Not at first. Not until she had flipped the side. Finally, when the needle clicked off she watched in amazement as Sooty twitched her tail and slinked into the garden, not remotely interested in anything else.

A few weeks later Snowy had trailed Sooty in through the door. Although, let's be straight, this was in fact Snowy the first. For there were many that were to follow him. A regal puss with pink eyes and a tail that was brown at the tip, she recognised soon enough the spirit of her husband in him. Snowy liked to play Scrabble. Not with actual words, as David had done. But in cat form, now, he preferred to paw and play with the pieces. And that was enough for both of them.

After Snowy came Tabby, her mother, with an appetite for game – mostly of the pigeon variety. All slanty eyes and affection, Tabby would purr on her lap and sleep on her pillow, her tail stroking Norah 's thinning hair, just as her mother had done years before.

Ginger was a Canadian airman she had met during the war. Wild, picky and mischievous, he'd had a thing for the Andrews Sisters which, post-mortem, expressed itself in a preference for Choosy cat food and an insistence that she didn't sit under the apple tree with anyone else but him.

There followed a steady stream: Grey-boy, an English teacher for whom she held great affection; Socks, a black cat with white legs so very like her departed cousin Oliver; Raj, her friendly neighbour who'd got run over the previous year. He'd come back as a beautiful Siamese who was very, very affectionate. Albert, on the other side of the cottage, went some time back in the eighties. He'd been a gardener. Now he was a cheeky stray. Fluffy was her father, with long whiskers and a penetrating glare. And she received regular visits from Tiger, Misty, Edward, Sukie, Oscar – too many sometimes to count. All her friends and family, returning.

When Snowy the Fourth had died she had been bereft and had to force herself into the night to dig him a decent grave. Though no more Snowys had come recently, she knew, at some point he would return.

Therefore it was really no surprise when, after the Queen's speech and the pudding had gone down, she swivelled her eyes to the white shadow at the door.

It meowed loudly.

And Norah smiled.

Angling her weary bones out of the chair she opened the windows to let New Snowy in. Blond and calm with a gleam in his eyes, he stubbornly refused to enter.

Instead he retreated into the inches-thick white lawn.

And stared with familiar pink eyes.

'Follow me,' he purred into her head.

How could she refuse such an offer?

Leaving the house in her bedclothes, she waded into the slush.

There was no coldness out here either.

And no paw prints, she noted, as she followed his path.

That's odd, she thought and checked behind her.

But no.

There was nothing back there either.

No tread.

No footprints in the snow.

Just an old lady sleeping in the armchair, surrounded by cats, so very wrinkled and baggy at the seams.

'Meow,' the white cat beckoned.

When she turned back to him she saw, to her surprise, that there was nothing but brightness.

Everything was white.

The purest of colours.

David had, at last, come to take her.

THE HOUSE ON
SAVAGE LANE

'Sorry about that. Mother is very old and given occasionally to fits.'

'Yes, the screaming. I do apologise. The medication has calmed her now. She'll not disturb us again. She does get rather over-excited when a traveller passes by. You see we're so out of the way, custom rarely favours us these days. The misfortune of your motorcar breaking down in the lane is, indeed, our great fortune.'

'What's that? Oh no. Kind of you but I shall be eating shortly. Would not want to ruin my appetite. Though please do go ahead. But I'll have a drink. Would you care for a glass of my special mulled wine? Here, let me fill you.'

'It does, does it? I fear I was a little too free with the cinnamon. That's it, drink up. Oh no, there is plenty more.

'Now, are you sure you want to hear the story? It unsettles most. Some have fled the house in terror once hearing the tale. Rest assured, in most cases, I have managed to safely return them to the warmth of our humble abode.'

'Yes you're right. I am being modest – it *is* a fine house, indeed. We are lucky.

'So the story ... You do? I see. If you're absolutely sure ... Very well. Draw in close, throw another log on the fire if you will. It's a chill night. I shall just add some of that coal.

'Now this may take quite a while so settle in. All right? Then I'll begin.

'It all started with the birth of Miss Cordelia Dorcroft. The youngest of five children and the only girl. From the word go her parents could see there was something very special about Cordelia. As a baby she displayed the sweetest of natures, crying very little and smiling oftentimes. And as the years passed it became evident that this loveable child was becoming a very charming young woman. Her beauty was not limited to her features, for she was gifted with an exceptionally handsome figure and a radiant face. An inner light seemed to shine from Cordelia and was remarked upon by many, including the parson who took her under his wing and tutored her in the works of the Lord.

'In this way Cordelia became a pious woman, often sighted nursing the sick, providing comfort to the poor. There was some talk of her joining an order but, as is often the way, her father, Major Dorcroft, was an astute man and could quite clearly see potential for a good marriage, and one which, if engineered correctly, might secure his own growing status in society.

'Now, as we know, where light shines brightest, shadow also falls. And as it was, on the other side of the village lived another family by the name of Barren-Barton. An old family, they had prospered for centuries and were treated with due accord by both the village and wider society.

'To the Barren-Bartons were born three sons. The eldest was established in London, having married a nobleman's daughter and produced two well-mannered grandchildren for his parents to adore. The youngest, too, had shown an aptitude for study and attained a position at the Royal Observatory. The middle son, Thomas, however, did not live up to the expectations of the family. His was an ill-tempered and fierce disposition. Known to frequent the gaming tables, he had brought no small amount of shame upon his father, who had on numerous occasions been required to settle his errant son's debts. And Thomas had what you'd call a fascination for the ladies, some of whom were more than willing to take up with him. For along with dashing good looks, the young man also possessed an aspect of wild, untethered excitement, touched with dangerous passion, that was undoubtedly of interest to the more careless of females, perhaps themselves with an eye on a marital settlement. However, their hopes were never fulfilled, Thomas desired no wife to bind him, and Barren-Barton Senior was compelled on occasion to compensate their situations with a measure of gold.

'There was, all agreed, a mighty arrogance to the middle son, an understanding of which he had assured himself, that his father's money would resolve any problems he created. And so that was, to a certain extent, how he became accustomed to living.

'Now, Thomas's appetites were ordinarily strong, his manner reckless and unthinking, but when fuelled by drink, which was frequent, they would grow uncontrollable and unleash the foul character that his black soul had become. And so it was, on one of these occasions that Fate threw Cordelia into his path.

'Thomas had never made a secret of his desires, and the customers of the local inn were well aware of his professed achievements as seducer, and of his ambitions to corrupt the pure. Cordelia's name had of course been mentioned on many occasions, for such was the great virtue of the young woman that her name had become a legend of the locality.

'It was returning from the inn, one dark and dismal winter evening, that Thomas came across Cordelia. She had been tending to a family stricken with fever and had stayed longer than anyone thought wise.

'One can only imagine what happened that dreadful night and I won't detail what occurred, but suffice it to say, one of Thomas's long held-desires was sated.

'The next day, while he bragged and boasted at the inn, doctors tended to Cordelia. Her injuries were severe and it was feared that she might not survive them. But after two long weeks the dear girl opened up her eyes.

'Her recollection of the crime had almost been wiped from her mind and perhaps in time she may have been able to return to some semblance of a normal life, were it not that Fate had another blow to deal her: soon she found she was with child.

'This was a great tragedy not only for the girl but her parents too, who had held their hopes high for their only daughter. There was some talk of the culprit being brought to justice, but a hastily convened meeting between Mr

Barren-Barton and Major Dorcroft achieved an outcome more appealing to both: Cordelia was to be wed to Thomas. It was a match that in other circumstances may have been a celebration. Yet for Cordelia it presented a cruel punishment.

'With the seed of her violator growing within she made her way down the aisle, fainted, and could only be brought to by the salts. Witnessed by the parents of the pair, the deed was over in minutes. After, transported to a fine, but isolated residence, Cordelia began her confinement.

'It was in autumn of the next year that, one stormy night, Cordelia endured a long and torturous delivery, finally birthing twins. The first was a healthy young boy, blessed with the fair complexion of his mother, perfect in almost every way. The second twin to greet the world could not have been more different. A dark, mewling, barely human thing, covered in coarse black hairs, it was wizened and wrinkled like an old man. The runt child's skin was red raw and it was deformed by an acute twisting of the spine.

'As is often the case with mothers, Cordelia's love was blind. She doted on the children equally, compared them to two turtle doves and consumed herself dutifully with their care. Any servant who looked askance at the second son was forthwith given notice to leave. So by their first year the household comprised of just one old maid, Ida, and a daily housekeeper.

'But to the father love did not come easy. Thomas could no longer bear the sight of his wife. Now ravaged by sorrow and labour, disfigured by his own assault, Cordelia had lost much of her outward beauty. Their offspring, too, revolted him, so he spent much of his time away from the house and returned very quickly to the lifestyle of his bachelor youth.

'For the first few years of their life, mother and children got along happily. It was when the twins turned five years of age and were given more freedom to roam that it was brought to Cordelia's attention that certain creatures were appearing in the boys' room: a magpie with no head, partially decaying; a young rabbit, its insides opened up and legs gnawed; a grey squirrel with no eyes, barely alive.

'It was clear to both maid and mother that the sins and perversions of the father had taken root in one of his children. This of course was no fault of the child, merely an unfortunate act of nature. It was agreed that Cordelia and Ida would be more alert to offence and seek to correct it when found.

'As the twins grew older, the discoveries grew ever more grotesque. Though there now seemed another hand involved – whenever a dissected creature would appear it would be part wrapped in bandages as if one of the children, the boy with Cordelia's nature, had attempted to repair the other's dark deeds.

'Upon questioning, neither the angel nor the devil would reveal who had done what. A secret pact had been formed by them to obfuscate their affliction – one needing to gnaw and wreck, the other compelled to heal; though Cordelia, knowing well both sons, saw which had inherited her character and understood, without judgement, that the other was tainted by the darkness of their father. But still so gentle and good was her own nature that she never favoured one above the other.

'And so the years passed by and while the essence of one became bright and sunny, the other was attracted to the morbid. As the middle years approached, the latter's turns and outbursts increased in violence and strength. By the time the twins reached thirteen, a system had been designed to thwart or, at times, restrict the episodes when his desires surfaced. In this, his ever-patient mother did achieve some success, understanding it was an instinct that could not be erased, only managed and redirected.

'But Cordelia could not be vigilant always.

'Having only a daily housekeeper and the maid to administer the home, she was often required to make excursions to town for clothes and medicines and provisions not available in the small village.

'It was upon returning from one of these journeys that Cordelia made the awful discovery that was to finally turn her mind.

'It being late in the evening, the housekeeper had left for the day, yet the maid was nowhere to be found. Their mistress searched high and low until eventually she reached the boys' room at the top of the house.

'Oh what terror she must have suffered when she beheld the scene within. In the corner, crunched up like a ball, one of the twins quivered and wailed. In the centre was the father's son. His teeth dripping with dark fluid, long sinewy tatters fluttering around his mouth. As she stepped closer

Cordelia saw the young man was gnawing on what was left of the maid's jawbone.

'Summoning what was left of her strength Cordelia bade her murderous son to go clean himself, then she turned to her other child and with much persuasion managed to soothe him, for he was very afraid. Lost in this ministration neither good child nor mother heard the commotion occurring downstairs until the door flew open and they saw Thomas Barren-Barton, eyes afire. Taking in the scene his mind burst loose and within seconds he had pulled his twisted son from his mother's arms and hurled him with such force at the wall that immediately the poor lad's head was split open. The coarse-haired, red-skinned angel-child died within Cordelia's embrace. This held no solace for the murderous brother who, though his passion for flesh and his tastes for darkness had appalled his hunchbacked twin, still loved him dearly. When he returned to the room freshly washed, he flew at his father.

'The next morning, when the housekeeper returned, she found three mangled corpses – old Ida, the maid, the hunchbacked twin and the chewed remains of his father.

'Poor Cordelia was found in the gardens walking like a somnambulist, her mind gone forever. And who was to doubt the account of the surviving son whose faltering cherubic face told of a robber who had attacked in the night?

'From time to time, thereafter, villagers would sometimes disappear, but they were useless people who served little purpose and who could be removed conveniently without occasioning a gap in good society.

'Decades passed and a new road was built. It thankfully

brought fresh faces by. Though locals would avoid the house at all costs, for they said, and still do, that on dark nights like this you could hear the dead ones' cries in these here lanes leading to the house.'

'I'm sorry old chap – can you repeat that again? Oh you feel cold? I'm not surprised. It has grown very dark, it's true.'

'I say, are you all right? You seem awfully pale. What's that? Where is the house?

'I thought I'd told you already – why it's here. This house. That's the ticket.'

'Cordelia? Yes, you've got it. She's my mother. No, please don't get up, you won't be able to anyway. Now, I believe you'll be joining me for dinner.'

EASILY MADE

It was brass monkeys and Janet was quick to tell Matt that she had been waiting outside the cottage for a good thirty minutes.

He was profuse in his apologies: lunch at the in-laws had over-run and he'd had trouble getting away.

Matt was new to social work. It would probably take him a couple more years to realise that being 'on call' on Boxing Day meant 'at work'.

'And then I went to Church Pass rather than Church Lane,' he finished, with a shrug.

Janet scowled.

'A simple mistake,' he bleated. 'Some are easily made.'

'Not really,' said Janet. Her fingers were numbing. 'It's about paying attention to detail. Church Lane is in the village. Church Pass is out by the cemetery.'

'As I found out,' said Matt trying to smile. 'Sorry,' he said again. 'I just assumed . . .'

'Well don't.' Janet cut him off. 'Don't assume. If in doubt – ask. That's what our job is all about – attention to detail. You need to learn this, Matt.'

'Yes, you're right.' Matt let his head hang, suitably chastised. 'To be honest, I hadn't thought we'd see much action today.'

Janet sighed. Boxing Day was always busy: old people tended to hang on over Christmas. Then, once they'd said goodbye to family members who'd gone to the trouble of visiting or hosting them for the festivities, they would let go. Of everything. Their worries, their dysfunctional bodies, their lives.

This one here, Norah, had been slightly different. She'd passed over some time yesterday afternoon or evening, according to the coroner. But her timing had been a little skewed because she was on her own. Although, Janet corrected herself, that wasn't entirely true. The neighbour, who popped in with a quiche for Norah on Christmas night, had phoned the police and informed them of her demise, adding that there were 'a lot of cats there'. The medical examiner had also noticed the abundance of Norah's feline friends and suggested Social Services should get them to the local animal refuge asap. So when Janet got the call she came straight away.

If she'd have known Matt was going to take as long as he had to get the keys and meet her in Adder's Fork, then she would have gone and got them herself.

But hindsight is a wonderful thing, she thought, as he jangled them in front of her.

'Let's get in then, shall we?' he suggested 'Do you know how many furry friends she had in there?'

Janet stopped herself from snapping that if she knew that

she would have gone to the refuge first and got the required number of cages. She just said, 'No, let's open up and see.'

Thankfully there was no smell of death in the place, no lingering odour of decay or leaked body fluids. You got it in some. She was grateful that this old girl had had a dignified exit, been found quite soon after and that the cats hadn't got hungry in the interim.

Janet did a quick tour of the upstairs and found it empty. The sparse furniture that remained had been covered in dust sheets, so they looked like ghosts of the old lady's memories. Norah had only used the ground floor of the cottage. The living room was multi-functional as bedroom, dining room and living room, too. Though it was full of furniture.

Matt eyed the comfy chair opposite the telly. It sagged deeply in the middle. Someone had sat there a lot. 'So sad, isn't it?' he said. 'That she spent Christmas on her own.'

But Janet shook her head. 'Some people like it like that. Christmas can be an awful strain.'

Matt, young and family-friendly, sighed. 'Well, I wouldn't want to end up like this.'

'She had her cats, Matt. Remember?'

He did. 'That's right. And I count three of them in here.' He pointed to a silver Siamese, a skinny ginger tom and one that was black over its body but pale round the legs, as if it were wearing white socks.

'Mmm,' said Janet. 'I'm not sure that these constitute "a lot".'

So she went into the kitchen. It was a lot yuckier in there. By the door sat a hairy brown cat with, what she'd call 'wide fur'. She wasn't a cat person, but this one looked comfy and cosy, exactly the kind of thing you'd want to cuddle up to on cold nights. It was settled on the doormat and, judging from the smell of things, was seriously incontinent. Perhaps, she thought, it had been waiting to be let out. Her heart contracted with an unexpected spasm of empathy for the poor old thing and she thought about opening the door but, just as quickly, remembered that cats were rather headstrong creatures and there would be no guaranteeing that if it got out, the tabby would come back when required.

She scurried over and bent down.

'Sorry dear,' she said to the fat tabby. 'We're going to have to take you away. But you'll be fine. It's a refuge. You can go to the loo there.'

She went to stroke it, but just as she extended her hand, the big furry ball leapt at her.

'Ow,' she yelped and withdrew her arm. The cat had clawed the flesh on her wrist.

'Oh you shrew.' She got up as it stood there making a funny noise and staring at her and went to the sink to run the wound under water. There was another one, entirely grey, patrolling the work surface. It came to the sink and looked at her.

'I hope you're not as bad mannered as your pal down there,' she said, and it promptly batted her with its paw.

It was a light movement and did not hurt her arm, though Janet's pride was injured. 'Excuse me!' she said with indignation and flicked some water at it. The grey, however, did not have much of a sense of humour. In fact, it must have been quite upset because before she had time to turn the tap off it had leapt at her and dug its paws in around her head.

'Gerroff! Gerroff!' she screamed and staggered back, hit the back door, heard the yowl of the incontinent tabby that had returned to its place there and tried to throw the grey off her. But it had sunk in its claws.

'Get off me!' she screamed and heard the interior door opening. Fast footsteps came into the room, though she still couldn't see where from.

'Good God,' yelled Matt. 'What did you do to it?'

'Do to it? Do to it? Nothing,' Janet snarled through the fug of grey fur.

She could feel the talons extending deeper into her hairline and knew they had broken the skin, for a trickle of warm blood was running down the side of her face. 'Get it off.'

'Stop moving,' said Matt.

And for once she complied.

'Now, now,' she heard his voice and had a mind to be angry with her colleague for being so conciliatory with the beast, but the claws began to slacken off.

'Come on, that's it,' Matt cooed. Soon he had slipped an arm under the grey's belly and gently slid it off her head.

When Janet finally opened her eyes, she saw Matt was holding the little demon on his chest.

'Come on now,' he cooed again. 'She's only trying to help. We both are. Don't hurt Mummy Janet.'

Oh God. He was a cat man.

He leant to the kitchen surface and inched the grey off

his chest. It prowled off into the shadows then sat down and began licking Janet's blood from between its toes.

'He's a beauty,' said Matt smiling – yes smiling! She couldn't believe it. 'A Russian Blue. Usually they're so passive.'

'Well that one is bloody well not!'

'They're disoriented,' said Matt. 'You need to remember that. They've just lost their mistress.'

Janet's compassion had shrivelled, 'Hmmm. So how many have we got?'

Matt looked back in the direction of the living room. 'Five, I think. Though there may be more outside. We'll have to come back.'

'If they're outside, then they can fend for themselves,' said Janet, well and truly peeved.

'She's cut into you.' Matt gestured to Janet's forehead. He pulled out a hanky from his top pocket. 'You might want to wipe it with this.'

She took it and held it to the scratch, which was starting to sting. She was allergic to cats.

'Right,' she said. 'That's five cages then.'

In the event, when they got to the refuge, the vet was full of frowns. He was also young and a bit surly and appeared to resent the fact that he had been plucked out of the family bosom on Boxing Day.

'Look,' he said. 'We've got no room at the inn. I hope you're aware.'

Matt and Janet looked at each other, not understanding the biblical reference.

The vet sighed. Social workers were so literal. 'There's no room here for any more referrals,' he translated. 'Christmas is our busiest time. You know – a pet's not just for Christmas? The advert? A lot of them don't even last the day with their new owners. And we're the dumping ground. In the past twenty-four hours we've received six dogs, four of them puppies left in a wheelie bin, three French hens (dumped in a bottle bank by some poetic arsehole), two kittens abandoned in a plastic bag, a couple of degus that came complete with cage, and a monkey. Don't ask. Oh yes and a poorly goat called Brian who was taped into an industrial waste bag and left in the alley out back.'

Janet tutted. 'Some people have no conscience.'

'Tell me about it,' said the vet.

'No room?' Matt repeated, just to be sure. 'No room here? But you told us to bring them at once.'

'That's right. And you can leave them here but they'll have to be put to sleep. Unless you can organise new homes for them? We can't.'

Even Janet was quite shocked by the bald statement. 'But it's Boxing Day. You can't expect us to organise alternative accommodation for five cats today.'

'Then I'm afraid, they'll have to go to the big cat basket in the sky,' said the vet. 'In the most humanitarian way, of course.' He smiled thinly. 'However, we only have four cages to transport them,' he said as an afterthought.

'What does that mean?' asked Matt.

The vet leaned on his metal table. 'Failed maths, did you? Two trips.'

*

It took them a while to get Norah's cats into the cages. They really did not want to go, and Janet experienced some small amount of shame as she and Matt shut the doors on each of them. But not that vicious Russian Blue. Oh no. Though Matt did the coaxing, it was Janet who triumphantly fastened the door on that little devil.

'I'll get the vet to start with you,' she said to it through its bars.

And he did.

They didn't want to hear or see Norah's cats making their way to cat heaven so as soon as the deed had been done with the malicious grey, they took its vacant cage and returned to the cottage.

There was only one left. The antique tabby with the fat hair.

Janet wondered briefly if she might be able to take it, but what with her allergies it wasn't a good idea.

'Maybe you've got room for that tabby?' she asked Matt as they pulled up outside the cottage again.

'The incontinent one, on the mat?' asked her colleague. 'Seriously? There is no way my wife would have her inside. But maybe the neighbour?' he said and jerked his head at the door.

A woman was waiting for them. She had a fake fur coat with her hair in a top knot. When she saw them she gave a wan smile. It had a semi-friendly edge to it.

'Good idea,' said Janet, hopefully.

As they approached the door with the remaining cage, the woman came forwards.

'Hello,' she said. 'The door was open. I hope you don't mind me coming over. I was on my way in. You've got my key.'

'Yes, that's right. It's Mrs Hope, isn't it?' said Matt. 'Sorry for not getting them back to you sooner. It's been a bit of a day.'

And they made their way into the living room. Janet placed the cage on the floor and, to her amazement, watched the fat tabby walk straight in.

'Indeed,' said Janet. 'What with all Norah's cats. We've had to go back and forth, back and forth.' And she touched the scratch on her hairline. 'Been a bit of a trial.'

The woman blinked. Her long-coated lashes batted up and down. Janet could smell her flowery perfume.

'Norah's cats?' said Mrs Hope, a big furrow developing between her eyebrows.

'Yes. We found five of them,' said Matt. 'Were there more?'

The woman shook out the wrinkles on her forehead and smiled. 'Oh Norah only had the one. This tubby little tabby, here. Bit of a handful, I always thought. But Norah absolutely adored her.'

'But,' said Matt. 'There were "lots". You reported lots. The medical examiner said there were lots. And we found them.' He gulped. 'Here.' His voice broke as he said, 'Her cats.'

Mrs Hope poked her hand through the cage and stroked the tabby. 'Oh no,' she laughed. 'Norah simply loved feeding all us neighbours' cats. Spent a fortune on cat food. We used to send meals round as payback, really. That's why I'm here. I thought I'd better collect my Sukie before it gets dark. Have you seen her? She's a Russian Blue?'

Matt's face was paling to match the fur of dearly departed Sukie. Under his nose small drops of perspiration had appeared.

'You know,' said Janet, her voice faltering. 'Some mistakes are easily made . . .'

IN THE BAG

Cliff finished polishing the brass urn and smiled to himself with mischief. He had missed a section, just below the lid, right at the front where a large pewter dove, its wings outspread, was borne aloft on a gust of hope, flying in peace to a new destination. Fluttering beneath it were three smaller creatures: two mockingbirds, he had been reliably informed by the undertaker, and a canary. All of which suggested peace in the afterlife but also formed an attractive decoration that enabled the urn to pass as an ordinary vase. Some people could be quite sensitive about ashes kept in living rooms, apparently. The three lesser birds he polished with zeal – it would please his wife to know he had taken some time to look after her mother's urn. But this bigger one at the top, well that was going to be left dirty. Just because he could. And no one would be the wiser.

He sat back, job done, and listened to the quiet.

A light breeze fluttered the curtains. Outside, in the street, a car backfired. The fridge in the kitchen hummed, spluttered then stilled. A letterbox flapped a few houses down. But apart from that there was nothing.

It was bliss.

At last.

What a relief.

If his mother-in-law had still been alive, it would be just about now that she would lean out of her deathbed in the spare room above him and call down in her rasping shrill voice: 'Cliff, dear, you've missed a bit.'

Which would prompt an involuntary response of much teeth gritting and buttock clenching followed by a polite riposte, 'Yes Doreen, quite right. Thank you so much.'

But his mother-in-law was dead.

Dead as a dodo, he thought and smiled again, imagining her with a large beak and feathers.

Dead as a doornail. He turned that over in his mind and came up with an image of her head on a tiny little screw. This also amused.

Dead as a dormouse. But no, he thought suddenly. Wasn't that *deaf* as a dormouse? Or was it deaf as a doorpost? He couldn't remember now but either description was entirely inappropriate for his mother-in-law. There was absolutely no way that Doreen could ever be considered even remotely hard of hearing. No indeed. On the contrary: Doreen Johnson's auditory range had been astonishingly extensive. On one occasion, when his nerves were slightly more frayed than usual, he caught himself wondering if, in fact, she was supernaturally enhanced. For his mother-in-law had been able to decipher every tiny squeak and bump so that she knew exactly what was happening in the house until the day she died. And, as such, was able to monitor his every move.

That is until she had just last month obligingly popped her clogs, been incinerated into ashes and brushed into the blue brass urn adorned with calling birds.

And now she was gone.

Cliff sighed. Contentedly.

See, there was no denying Doreen had been a trial of sorts. Though she'd never admit it to his face, Anne would have agreed too. Cliff's own brother had called her a 'formidable battle-axe', and a few other names he would never be able to repeat in front of his dear wife.

Personally, Cliff thought that battle-axe was another inaccurate description. Doreen had none of those assertive, stoic qualities that people associate with warriors, male or female. Hers was more of a passive aggression, often verbal, with a constant niggling undertone that had burrowed deep into Cliff's subconscious. During the last months of her illness, when she had been virtually bed-bound upstairs in the spare room, her voice had followed him around the house. She could hear the sounds he made and just *tell* what he was up to, despite the stairs and floorboards and carpet in between.

Whenever he'd put the kettle on there would be an 'Oh a nice cup of tea would be ever-so kind – if you can make time for a little old lady like me, which I expect you can't really, and why would you now you've got your feet nice and snug and under the table?'

Or when he'd load the washing machine, 'How is that model going, Cliff? Is it efficient? Isn't it quiet? I paid such a lot for it, you'd have expected no less. Happy though to help you out. What with your lack of income dear. Us Johnson women have always rallied when there's a weak link in the chain.'

When he'd hoover the carpets. 'You've missed a bit, Cliff. No it's fine. I'm happy to help. Don't worry – we all know it doesn't come naturally to a man. It's such a feminine instinct, you see, to nest. But the Duchesse 127 is a good vacuum. I know it's pink but then when I bought it I didn't think you'd be cleaning up after us girls' mess.' And the bloody thing looked like her too – with its pink body and grey spade-like handle. But he'd get those teeth gritted and those buttocks clenched and get on with the job in hand.

See, Doreen had always had a problem with house-husbands.

Anne had never expressed any kind of judgement about his status whatsoever. After their daughter Poppy was born, it had seemed the logical choice, given his wife's meteoric rise through Her Majesty's Judicial Service and his horizontal trajectory as a council plumber.

Not that it had always been that way.

He'd never intended to go into that line of work. Having studied Classics at Durham, he'd always had in the back of his mind a fuzzy idea that by forty he might be a successful professor, lecturing on Homer and immersing himself in archaeological digs in his spare time. But then he'd done the Australian travelling thing and fallen in love with the country. On his return to his frosty island home, he immediately set about researching how to emigrate over there and soon discovered the Lucky Country wanted plumbers galore.

In fact Australia was desperate for them. A visa was practically guaranteed.

Over the next couple of years he worked hard at two jobs and retrained in the evenings achieving a Merit for a Level 3 Diploma in Domestic Plumbing and Heating. He was about to book his flight when he met Anne at an Aussie pub in Earl's Court. She'd just got back from Sydney and had rocked up to the bar for a dose of irresponsible nostalgia before getting serious and grown up and tackling a starter job as a junior in a pre-eminent law firm.

One thing led to another then another and within eighteen months Anne was pregnant. The product of the make-up sex that had come after he announced he was going to Australia. But Cliff did the decent thing and cancelled his ticket. And the rest, as they say, is history.

It helped that Poppy just happened to be the best baby ever. And the best baby ever grew into the best little girl. And despite the fact he'd never boomeranged back to the Lucky Country, as he'd longed to, paternal love filled his heart and every fibre of his being so much that it cancelled out any negatives and, in fact, better than that, it made him feel proud.

Within another couple of years he'd put a ring on Anne's finger and bought them a modest but perfectly adequate semi in Essex, where they settled down and created a home.

The only real fly in the ointment was the mother-in-law he'd inherited. Doreen had never been impressed. A lower-middle-class widow with aspirations to the upper-middle and beyond, his mother-in-law's ambitions were thwarted by the untimely death of her spouse some thirteen years previously. A sudden heart attack while having lunch at the bank, brought on, Cliff believed, by the incessant demands of his wife. Frank Johnson was, at the time, grappling with a suffocating mortgage for an unnecessarily large four-bedroom house on a new development in Hertfordshire with its own Waitrose and shared green spaces, a holiday home in the Algarve and Anne's university fees.

Doreen was devastated. She had loved that house. Its high-end finish was the envy of all her friends. Frank's selfish expiration, however, forced her to face the consequences of the extraordinary debts her husband had conspired to conceal. But the creditors were unsympathetic and hungry for repayment, so the house and the apartment in Portugal were sold for a song. Doreen managed to eke out enough from the leftover change to purchase a two-bedroom flat in a neighbourhood with no parking and a Lidl. Anne took on student loans and then, upon graduation, hot-footed it off to Australia, which was pretty much as far away as she could get from her mother's moans.

Doreen raised her head above the grim reality in which she found herself, and became committed to living vicariously through her daughter. Her aspirations, however, were brought to a skidding halt when she was introduced to Cliff. And although Doreen constantly wielded her axe, attempting to sever the cords that strung the two lovers together, Anne was not to be deterred.

The wedding, whilst in a church hall wearing Blue Cross reductions from the Debenhams sale, surprisingly however appeared to soothe Doreen. Or perhaps she just gave up for a while. And by then the delightful Poppy was toddling her way into everyone's hearts, sweetening the sourest of lemons. For a time things floated on in a sea that was wavy but calm.

It was when she became ill and moved in with them that inevitably it all got worse. As a distraction to her growing pain, she fixated on Cliff's domestic chores, which is perhaps why he did so much of the buttock-clenching routine and didn't bite back, but let it go. Or tried to.

His stamina was remarkable.

In the mornings, at the squeak of a wheelie bin, he'd be issued with instructions to ensure he cleaned the receptacle after emptying – 'I don't know how you people can live like that?' Lunchtimes would elicit a lecture on the ills of microwaved food – 'Well, if you want to die of cancer, so be it.' The school run would produce comments concerning the unnaturalness of men who liked to linger about playgrounds – 'Pervs with nothing better to do.' He didn't need Windolene to clean the windows of an afternoon but vinegar – 'Nothing wrong with a bit of elbow grease, Cliff.' And if he got the Hoover out – 'You've missed a bit.'

And she was always friggin' right.

But in the final week he'd almost felt sorry for the woman: the death rattle, the tears, the saying goodbye. Then she'd gone, and although he tried to feel guilty and a bit sad about it, all he really noticed was a huge sense of relief lifting from his shoulders.

He felt it again now, as he put the urn back on the mantelpiece in the lounge, a smaller lift, true, but an appreciation of

Doreen's absence nonetheless. He wanted rid of the container to be honest – it was a reminder of Doreen's observations – but he'd agreed it could rest here until Anne decided where she should scatter her mother's mortal remains.

Which kind of made it look like he'd meant to do it, even though, honest to God, he so, so hadn't. Possibly somewhere in the recesses of his brain there might have been an impulse there but it definitely, absolutely, no way José, was a conscious thing.

The problem was that he'd got carried away with a couple of articles in the *Guardian* online and hadn't realised that the hour for school pick-up was approaching. He'd promised Poppy this morning that he'd get the Christmas decorations down from the attic before she got home and they could put them up together. So once he'd got into the loft and hurriedly brought the boxes down he'd thought he'd better make a bit of an effort. Seemed silly just to leave them there untouched.

He pulled out a big arrangement of fake pine cones and holly, entwined with silk lilies and red berries. If he stuck that on the mantelpiece it would immediately change the look of the room and bestow some seasonal cheer. So he'd lifted it up, but instead of moving the urn out of the way with his hands, he nudged it along the sill with the arrangement.

One of the silk flowers at the edge, however, which he thought was flexible, turned out to be supported by a wooden stick, and unfortunately it was this that knocked into the side of the big blue brass urn.

Cliff watched with horror as the urn tottered sideways, then leant forwards and keeled, before it began to pitch off the edge. Cliff, his reflexes slightly lethargic at this late hour, attempted to tap it back onto the shelf, but he miscalculated and slapped the urn lid, which ricocheted back to the wall, leaving the contents unprotected. He could only watch, open-mouthed, as the mortal remains of his mother-in-law sprayed out of the somersaulting urn and scattered across the shag pile below.

Quickly Cliff fell to his knees, up-righting the urn and picking up bits of grey sand in his fingers, foolishly trying to stick the grains back inside.

But it was no good: the damage was done. As he tried to rub the ashes away they caught into the carpet, staining it a deep shark-grey.

And it was everywhere.

There was only one thing for it, he thought, noting the time. He got out the Duchesse 127 and sucked the dark dust from the carpet, the surrounding hearth and sill. And though this time he did feel quite a measure of guilt, when he sat back and unplugged the Hoover, there was no spilled Doreen anywhere to be seen.

He thought he had probably just about got away with it.

'You've missed a bit' a voice said.

Cliff froze.

He knew that tone. The niggling superiority meshed with a dose of spleen.

'Over there, by the poker.' It came again.

Cliff gasped, as his eyes fixed on the source. The voice was coming from the Hoover.

'Over there boy, you've got eyes haven't you?'

And perhaps unfastened by horror or defaulting into his prior subservience, he ran his eyes over the place where the poker lay. Damn! The Hoover was right – there was a little patch of death-grey ashes underneath its stand.

Without consciously registering what he was doing, Cliff picked up the vacuum cleaner and sucked up the last offending splat of dust.

Then he sat down and looked at the vacuum cleaner, but it wasn't saying anything anymore.

Poppy was just delighted to be putting the decorations up with her dad and did not notice his furtive glances at the Duchesse 127 in the corner of the room.

Nor did Annie see or hear anything unusual in the lounge, which led Cliff to believe that the stress of Doreen's passing and the shock of the untimely urn accident had contrived to cause aural hallucinations.

So it was with a jaunt in his step the following morning he kissed his wife goodbye, scooped Poppy up for the school run and returned home to celebrate his wonderfully empty house with a nice cup of coffee.

But as soon as the kettle had boiled, he heard it.

'Oh, a nice cup of tea would be ever-so kind.'

His hand paused in mid-air, the spoonful of instant dangling over the counter.

He breathed in.

He looked behind him.

Nothing.

'Although why would you now you've got your feet nice and snug and under the table?'

It came from the hall.

Slowly, feeling the air around him tense and sharpen, he turned his eyes to face the sound.

Something bleeped. Although ...

That wasn't a cough, was it?

His heart sped up.

No. How . . .?

For there in the hallway, staring at him, was the Duchesse 127.

Cliff dropped the coffee spoon on the floor sending the dark grains scattering across the tiles.

He took a step towards the vacuum cleaner and touched it to make sure it was real.

It was.

His hand recoiled for a moment then in one fell swoop scooped up the Hoover, ran down the hallway with it in his arms and then chucked it out the front door.

It was bin day tomorrow. Thank God.

That would be the end of that.

Doreen and her demonic Hoover would no longer infest this house. Dust pans and brushes had served Britons well for hundreds of years and would do for him just as well.

And it was this thought that sustained him throughout his chores.

He was slightly uncomfortable about the fact that he had disposed of his mother-in-law's ashes in such an indecorous manner but, he reasoned, this was surely the awkward truth that had conjured the voice.

Yes, that was the most logical explanation. It was guilt of course that haunted him rather than his mother-in-law's spirit reincarnated into a vacuum cleaner.

Now he thought about it, he could see how absurd he had been.

And a cackle of laughter tripped over his tongue and he shrugged his shoulders and decided to make a very special dinner for Anne and Poppy tonight.

And certainly his efforts did not go unappreciated. In fact, Anne informed Cliff he could have a lie-in and she would take Poppy to school in the morning.

So, it was a perfectly rested Cliff who stretched his body as he came lolloping down the stairs to find, at the bottom, the Duchesse 127 glaring at him again.

On its handle there was a Post-it. Cliff recognised his wife's writing: 'Why is this outside? It still works.'

Goddammit.

'Us Johnson women have always rallied when there's a weak link in the chain,' the vacuum cleaner said.

No, no, no.

This was not real.

Cliff took a breath and popped his head out the door. The Davidsons were having a conservatory built and there was a skip on the road outside.

Without changing his pyjamas or slipping on shoes Cliff picked up the Duchesse and, after charging down the road, threw the rogue cleaner into the skip, adding a two-fingered salute as she crashed onto the splintered wood and glass.

He brushed his hands.

No more bloody Doreen. No more. The skip was full now, which meant the builders would have to take it away soon and the Duchesse would be escorted to her proper resting place somewhere in a landfill site near the M25.

'I'm happy to help,' pleaded the Hoover.

But Cliff shook his head and shouted back, 'No you're not. Good riddance is what I say.'

Once inside, feeling suddenly unclean, he jumped in the shower, only becoming aware as he shampooed his hair that there was someone knocking on the door.

Guarded and unsure, he threw on a towel and went downstairs.

Oh God, he thought as he opened the door and saw Sam Davidson standing there with the Duchesse 127 in his hands.

'Look mate,' said Sam. 'I don't want to be funny, but we've paid for that skip and we've got a lot of rubble to get in there today. If you want rid of this, take it to the tip.' And he put the Duchesse down on the matt and closed the front door.

'Perv,' said the hoover, eyeing Cliff's towel. 'With nothing better to do.'

'Right! That's it!' yelled Cliff and he raced upstairs and threw on some clothes.

It was possible, he thought, that he was attracting some attention as he strode down Southend Pier in mismatched shoes, with hair full of soap suds and the Duchesse 127 in his arms. But he cared not one jot. Doreen was going to find herself sinking into a watery grave. One from which she could never return.

When he reached the end, by the fishermen, there were a few who cast quizzical glances, but most people looked away.

So there weren't many who witnessed Cliff get Doreen onto the railings and then push her into the drink.

'I paid such a lot . . .' she screamed and gurgled 'for . . .' splutter . . . 'it . . .' and she began to sink.

Cliff watched until the waves took down the plug and the last of the bubbles had popped on the surface of the sea . . . glug, glug, glug.

He had one nightmare about a zombie Hoover emerging from the estuary half-covered with seaweed and a determination to make its way back to their house, but other than that, he had enjoyed perfect peace since the pier episode.

With the advent of Christmas he became involved in preparations for the big day. The house was festooned with decorations, his mood began to climb. In fact, he had even caught himself in the living room mirror dotting crackers about the tree with a happy grin on his face. There was much to do and thus he was able to sink his unease into shopping for presents and the Christmas dinner he was cooking for his perfect little family and that of his brother's, who were joining them for the day.

So, it wasn't until everyone had gone that Christmas night, after Poppy had reluctantly climbed into bed, that he and

Anne found time to exchange their gifts, sitting cross-legged and slightly tipsy in front of a roaring hearth.

He had bought his wife her favourite perfume and some silk underwear, which she loved and declared she'd get into at once. Or at least after she had given Cliff his gift.

It was a large square box and heavy, too.

Although when he opened the lid and saw the hoover inside, he paused.

'What's up darling?' Anne cried. 'I know the last vacuum had to be chucked. Is it too boring?' she asked.

Cliff prodded it. Not a Duchesse 127, at least, he lifted it out of the box. It was squarish in shape and very male in appearance. In fact, it had a man's face painted on it.

'It's a Henry,' said his wife. 'And it works, too. I tried it out earlier, right here where we're sitting.'

But Cliff blanched.

Was he mistaken or was Henry's smile broadening into a leer?

'Happy to help out,' it cried.

JOCELYN'S STORY

I could tell you a thing or two 'bout my soon-to-be-ex-husband and not much of it would be pretty. Saying that, even I had to admit, as I looked out the window this morning, ole Ron was starting to develop great taste in broads.

His latest flame was a knockout.

About time.

Stretched out across the black sedan. With her tight little butt perched up on the wheel hub, she displayed herself perfectly well. I watched a white butterfly dance about her skirt before she waved it away.

There it was again. My friend.

This chick had a pleasing style to her dress. She had on this poppy-red summer frock and a matching choker.

Clever girl. Brought out her lipstick and she had good lips, too: plump and young and fleshy.

There was no bust to speak of but that had never bothered Ron.

Ron was a leg man.

'Come away from the window, Rita.' Mama tried to imply

there was some vague maternal concern going on. But she never got the tone right. 'You'll just upset yourself.'

I ignored her and let out a low whistle. 'Will you take a look at the pins on that.' Mama's gaze cottoned on to Ron, who now was wrapped around one of the most exquisite calves I'd seen in a hell of a long time. The new gal's proportions were exceptional. The curve of her ankle a pale crescent that hung like a waxing moon in the satiny black sky of Ron's chinos.

The knee was a little bumpier than I liked but that could be sorted.

'Don't start,' Mama fretted. 'Come away.'

But I could not take my eyes off the ankles, no siree. By my reckoning they had to be under eight inches all round. *Well done, Ron*, I thought, but didn't say it out loud for fear of upsetting Mama.

Though I couldn't help asking her, 'Do you think they'll be all right for …?'

I didn't have to finish.

She knew what I meant.

It made her shiver.

And *that* made me laugh.

No guts, that woman. Got all my strength from Pa, God rest his soul. A hard man, but he did well for the family. Some folks thought him too severe. I appreciated his single-minded dogma even if I didn't understand it as a child.

Mama coughed. I could tell she was trying to stand up to me. Her voice went low. 'I said don't start, Rita. I mean it. I'll leave.'

She hadn't fixed my tea yet so I didn't say no more and let her pull me away.

I've never been what you'd call domestic. Suzetta, the housekeeper, had moved when Ron upped sticks and I'd not yet found a replacement. I find the Help come so fussy these days.

There had been a couple of engagements, but the women hadn't lasted long.

Though it irked me to say, I was grateful that Irma, with her pustulating face and fierce body odour, had stuck around to do the household chores. The girl was a slut of a cleaner: skimming hours, missing corners, sweeping dust under rugs. You know the type. But she did the basics. And she kept her mouth shut, which was the main thing. Needs must when the devil drives.

And, we all know, he sure had driven me. It's usually one or the other ain't it. Don't know when the ole King of the Underworld, Beelzebub, I don't know when he started messing with me, putting ideas in this little ole head of mine.

If I had to put an age on it then I'd say it was maybe the same time that I realised I had certain attractions. I have always been one for excellence, never wishing for second best.

Didn't wise up to my qualities – girls don't – till freshman year when Joey McStride told me, square to my face.

'Rita,' he said. 'Anyone ever told you, you got the eyes of Betty Grable? Lips too,' he said and leant in to kiss them.

I ducked and swerved away from him. Now don't get me wrong, I'd puckered up for boys of all sorts by then and Joey weren't too bad. But it struck me that if this were true, then

I could raise my game. And by quite a stride too. I mean, I knew I was pretty – but Betty Grable?

'You're just teasing me, Joey,' I told him. 'That ain't fair.'

'No way, Rita. Tommy said it just the other day. And Buzz said so too.'

'They did?'

'Sure. You're our very own Swillen Valley pin-up.'

If I could have blushed I would. I didn't kiss Joey back but I let him feel my brassiere. The boy had earned it.

Back home in the mirror that night I saw what he meant. There *was* something of the star in me. Though my hair let me down. Betty weren't no mouse.

The very next afternoon I stopped by the drugstore and picked up a bottle of bleach.

Ain't never looked back since then.

After the hair came the wardrobe. Some showy frocks and tailored suits. I had my nose seen to. And once that healed there was no stopping with the guys. They flocked to me in herds much the same as they did to Betty. I picked out the best to confer my favours. And when I say 'best' I mean those that could do the best for me, of course – the richest, the ones with spare apartments and maids for the picking. Soon I was dining in only the finest restaurants, spending my days in the beauty parlour and my nights in the swankiest of clubs. I went to the races regular, owned five gold rings and holidayed beside the ocean.

By twenty-six I was the only girl on the block to own her own condominium. Well, have it bought for me. It's the same kind of thing.

You'd have thought I was as happy as Larry. But no, there was something that bugged me raw. See, I may have had the face of Grable but from the waist down things weren't so fine.

It was the legs.

Some folk might have said Betty's legs were a gift from God not to be coveted, just admired. But not I – the Devil was driving me remember – and he also desired Grable's legs.

The early procedures were fine. I had surgeons work on my thighs: a mole removed from my left leg. Weren't much of a mark but it was an imperfection, all the same. *I* knew it was there. Then a little shaping about the knees – some fat out of here, a squirt added there. My ankles were shaved down a touch to smooth the silhouette.

After my eighth operation I could boast Betty's vitals – 18.5" thigh, 12" calf and a couple of dainty 7.5" ankles.

Thing was, I was damned if I could increase the length. Scores of surgeons had told me it couldn't be done. Of course, there *were* ways, but these guys were too damn chicken shit to have a good go. 'Not for cosmetic reasons,' they whimpered like babies.

I needed someone who was willing to take a risk. Go the extra mile in pursuit of perfection.

But who?

It weren't like that when me and Ron first met. Though I should say when I got hold of Ron, seeing as the poor fool had no choice in the matter. The word 'met' suggests we arrived in each other's sphere purely by chance.

I'd always been the kind of gal who, once she knew what she wanted, didn't let nothing, and I mean nothing, stand in her way. Not that there was much obstructing my advance on Ron, the like of whom I had seen off many times before. No competition at all.

When I spied Ron I had the world, an army of young men and two sugar daddies at my feet. It was a few months after the ankle procedure. At that time I was so proud of my balls of comely flesh I glowed all over. There was a tiny indentation a half-inch above the right talus: a little blotch formed by chance into the shape of a star. Now Betty, she didn't have no flaws, it's true, but this dainty nick of ruby red flesh pleased me. I saw it to be a reminder that my fortune, my destiny, my guiding star, was my legs. One day I would be rewarded for my investment, effort and pain. And then I would become another ascending star.

When I found out Ron was a surgeon, li'l tears of joy splashed over my cheeks.

I watched him twirl this dumb broad on the floor. She weren't much to look at – some cheap Latino gold digger who made a thing of slamming shots in the piano bar. I liked the curl of Ron's lip, the width of his wallet and his sleek Clark Gable looks.

Gable and Grable.

We was verging on poetry.

I had to have him.

And it didn't take long for an obliging sailor friend to dispense of the gold digger so Lucky Boy Ron was freed up to receive my attentions.

Now I'd seen how the cleavage didn't work on him, unlike most barflies that drooled in my direction. So I slit my skirt right up to the thigh, angled my butt against the piano and thrust out my legs. They soon caught his eye. Then his hand, then his legs.

'Beautiful work,' he whispered the first night he took me to his home, a pink rambling villa called *Shangri-La*. Then he walked his fingers up my thighs, skating over the fading ghost-lines and scars.

It was a powerful coupling, anyone could see. We pleasured ourselves for nights and days. I enchanted Ron. I made myself indispensable to him. I pandered to his every whim, and some weren't so nice. But it came good: a few months on, he moved me out of the condo and into his mansion. After that it didn't take much to convince him of the importance inherent in lengthening my calves.

My good husband found some Russian quack experimenting out in Siberia. So we sent out some dollars and invited him to visit *Shangri-La*. He was eager enough for the money and could not get over my presentation to him as a willing specimen for experimentation.

Not that he was convinced by the idea. Not at first. But after a while, when he realised it wasn't a set-up, he agreed to start work. We sorted out a visa and, hey presto, within weeks he started breaking my bones.

I won't be bothering you with the details.

Suffice it to say, for a long year of my life I was immobile – splintered, crushed, grafted, stretched. Finally, my legs were caged into submission. The following May I took a break from surgery so I could debut my works in progress at the White Tie society ball.

Now the smart ones amongst you might have figured something went wrong else I wouldn't be sat here looking out at Ron scooting off with another cheap girlfriend.

Well, you could say it did. Though the work was priceless and awe-inspiring, some said, so too were those legs as brittle as a Ming vase.

I didn't care. I was moving towards my prize. One inch more and I would be complete.

The night before the ball I was feeling a mite playful and chanced to fetch some liquor from the cellar. It was usually off limits: those steps being sharp-angled, but Ron weren't back to watch over me, and I had a taste for it and what Rita wants, Rita gets.

I was usual so careful but as I touched the second stair my right knee locked and I tumbled down those thirteen stone mothers like a porcelain doll.

Screwed up my right leg so bad that, after he'd fixed the kneecap, even Ron could do no more.

'No,' he said. 'Rita, you gonna have to leave it be now.'

I was beside myself.

Can you imagine? One inch off my goal.

I can tell you I bawled.

I can tell you I cried and shrieked.

But none of you could know how much I was twisted up inside. It was outrageously unfair.

I mean – one inch!

Tormented and sore as hell I retreated to the poolside. Spent long weeks on the day bed, refusing company, listening to the agonised moans of Garbo on the gramophone. There is something unutterably exquisite in the nuances of Greta's melancholy. She provided some form of solace for Betty's elusive dimensions.

Then, just when I think there ain't anything left to hope for, God, or more likely the other one, shines a light at the end of the tunnel in the form of the stinking Lucy-Mae.

She replied to a 'Help Wanted' sign we'd put up in the window of a store on the main drag of town. We didn't want no paper trail. You'll understand why.

Now I know the homeless kind are usually full of disease and lice but I could tell Lucy-Mae was only just coming on to the bum's life. She stank like an alley-cat – piss and stale liquor, her teeth were going, her eyes were long weighed down by disappointment and wrinkled skin. Yet Lucy-Mae, tramp though she was, had the nearest damn proportions to Betty's legs I had ever seen.

Once we'd had her cleaned up she looked almost human. Never could get her off the liquor, mind. And sometimes I wonder if that was the problem – all that whisky-drenched tissue.

I'll never know for sure.

I made a big thing of measuring her statistics, for a uniform or such. She didn't make a fuss. Desperate, she was, for work. That girl had a haunted look about her. Both me and Ron could see she was running from something.

She was perfect.

Took us some time to convince her of the deal. But I could be persuasive, and Ron? Well, the man was rich enough to offer up a very juicy carrot. In the end she yielded to the promise of a one-way ticket to Veracruz and enough cash to drown herself in a pool-sized vat of bourbon.

So when we tell Doctor Rusky the idea he nearly wets his pants. Does the usual sermon about ethics and moral responsibility, but we could tell the damn fool just wanted a higher fee.

Once he'd had his first payment there weren't no issue 'bout getting him on board. He was as eager as me.

One dark night before Christmas he settled down to his final task. The sky was black and silent, the breeze whispering sweet nothings. I watched the baubles on the tree sparkle in the tinsel and thought of the wondrous gift that was coming, as pure and sweet as baby Jesus himself. Then I said goodbye to my darlin' Ron and took the ether down into my lungs.

As I faded into darkness the doc sliced off Lucy-Mae's legs and grafted them onto my stumps.

It was a long recovery but when I woke later I could see Santa had brought me the best present ever.

I had them. At last.

Couldn't use them, but that was by the by. The thought of their perfection kept me buzzing through the pain. I finally had Betty Grable's legs.

I watched them.

I stroked them.

I cleansed them.

Ron made love to them.

But.

Those damn legs, they didn't want me.

They say mind rules over matter but that's a God-awful lie. The harder I tried to keep them the more they rejected me.

Within weeks they were seeping pus from the scars. Putrefying under my very nose. The smell kept Ron away and soon the maid was refusing to dress the wounds. When Doctor Rusky got a whiff of septic flesh he shot off back home and sank back into obscurity in the Siberian plains.

I began fitting.

My temperature shot higher and higher.

Ron told me, most directly, 'Rita, the legs just have to go.'

I knew it though I didn't want it so.

Thing was, the whole Lucy-Mae thing hadn't of course been completely above board. It was sticky, so to speak. But Ron couldn't do no more on his own. We needed professional help.

That's when we hit upon the idea of a crash. So late March, I doused myself with the last of Lucy-Mae's stash, strapped on my seatbelt and drove to the garage at a speed fast enough to destroy the T-Bird.

And half of me.

There was a lot of weeping when I came round at the hospital.

None of it mine.

'We had to amputate. I'm sorry, Rita,' the doctor said, as pale as a scraped bone.

'It's all right, I know.' I smiled at Ron.

He couldn't meet my gaze; there was a hint of regret at his brow but then he pushed out his chin and looked at Mama. Resolve was written across his features for all to see.

'You're awful brave.' The doctor regularly regarded me with awe.

'There's always hope,' I replied to the poor man and patted his hand.

Ron coughed into his handkerchief and wiped his brow. We both knew it wouldn't be long before I had another pair of perfect pins sewn on.

There were sacrifices to be made though, I knew that for sure. So it came as no surprise when, three months later, he told me he had to leave. Of course I could see he didn't want to go, but I was healing. While I was confined to my wheelchair, only he could go out and find me new flesh. He had to get out into the world, of course. It was the price he had to pay – for the pursuit of my perfection.

There had been some horror shows over the past year. One girl, Italian I believe, had dark, swarthy skin. I said, 'Ron, you can't expect me to have mismatched legs. My face is white, Honey. I'd look like a keyboard and Betty certainly weren't that.'

She didn't last long after.

There was a stumpy brunette and a dwarf-like waitress who I gave short shrift. Don't get me wrong – the girls were stunning. Like I said, Ron had acquired good taste. But the legs weren't right: too short, too dark, not enough of the moon in the calf.

I had started to despair. Until today.

Ron had dropped by on the pretence of signing divorce papers.

'I'm moving on, Rita,' he said and purposefully patted my hand. 'She's outside.'

I'd winked at him. I understood.

And boy oh boy hadn't he done well? The legs were practically perfect. I watched them hop into the sedan and cruise down the stretch onto the open boulevard.

I was starting to get excited again.

'Mama!' I called into the kitchen. She appeared at the door with a tea cloth in her hand. 'Oh Ma, why don't you call out for some champagne? I feel like celebrating!'

Mother narrowed her eyes. 'I'm glad you're feeling better, love. It's time. Not sure I can stretch to the proper stuff. But I can nip down and get some fizz from Tesco?'

For a moment the hard consonants of her last word jolted me back. I blinked. I hated it when she did that. And suddenly it was as if someone had wiped a stained cloth over my view, dirtying my vision. Before I realised what was going on in my brain, the purple bougainvillea warped and faded. Too soon came the toxic grey and, without so much as a doff of my pill-box hat, my beautiful dream dissolved.

For three, four awful seconds I registered the urine-stained entrance to the block opposite. Fag butts on the floor mingled with syringes. The junky in the stairwell moaning with the wind.

No way. Not me. I was never going back there. Not to the dirt and the grime and the depraved lies of reality. Such seedy hopelessness could not be countenanced in one so special as I. There was no satisfaction to be gained, no point to the recognition and acceptance thereof.

No.

That is, rather, no siree.

My life was not here.

It was back.

Back there, where the breeze and cocktails came at sunset, served beside a kidney-shaped pool.

And so I closed my eyes and wheeled away from the view.

With one deep breath I returned to the swing in the lilac-scented garden with the ferny shrubs, in the balmy breeze, beneath the Milky Way. And somewhere before me that white butterfly fluttered.

Hope, I believe, is its name.

DEATH BECOMES HER

In between the ebb and the flow, the ceaseless repetitions and rhythms of life, death and destiny stalk us. Scientists, priests, astrologers and mathematicians know this. Stacey Winters knew it too. Though, out of all the cops in the City of London, it would quite probably be true to say, she had the hardest time dealing with death.

Tonight, off-duty and off-guard, a little too stressed and a touch too garrulous, she had let this truth escape her lips at the station's Social Club. So now she was being reassured that she wasn't unique in her reaction to death and decay; that *none* of her fellow officers had an easy time of it; that each and every policeman and woman, though they may appear untouched by the sight of a corpse, yes, each and every one of them was *always* shaken by the experience. They didn't get used to it as such, her colleagues agreed, they just got wise to their reaction. Thus distress became more manageable. Smaller.

'You see,' said her sergeant, in a confidential whisper, 'people say that it's love that separates us from the animals, but it's not. We can't be sure of much in life, but we all know we're going to die. No other species on the planet knows it, right? Dogs don't. Cats don't. Just us. And because we know it – we fear it. I don't know why we're afraid of a fact,' her boss continued, 'but I can give you some advice about what to do with fear. You control it, Stacey. That's what you do.'

Sergeant Edwards tapped the side of his nose. 'You can't let death control you or you'll be no good as a copper. No Stacey, you confront it, face it, stare it straight in the eyes. Overcome it. Not straight off, but gradual-like.'

But Stacey snorted. She meant to laugh, but it came out down her nose. Quickly she converted it into a cough to spare the sergeant's blushes.

Thing was, you didn't control Death by staring it in the eyes.

As if.

She should know: she'd stared it out more times than Sergeant Edwards had had cold shivers. She and The Reaper were practically on first name terms for God's sake. Death, actually, was the reason she'd joined the Force in the first place – to try and foil it.

It wasn't Edwards' fault that he was oblivious to this, so Stacey shrugged her shoulders, took a large swig of her drink and grimaced, remembering the first time she'd seen Death, way back in the fifth form at High School. She was fifteen and studying Classics. Her teacher, an enthusiastic recent graduate prone to unusual teaching practices, would quite often bring such dusty subjects to life by acting out small tableaux, showing videos, doing quizzes and such. She was brilliant like that, Stacey recalled, quite different to the dry, didactic monologues they were used to. No, Ms Topping, it had to be said, was her favourite. On this particular day, she was instructing the class on Roman attitudes to life and death, describing, rather vividly, the glorious returns of triumphant generals to the city of Rome: 'As they paraded into the city, waving to the cheering crowds from their glittering gold chariots, someone, wearing a death mask and costume, would stand by the generals' shoulders whispering softly into their ears, "Man, remember you will die," so that, even at moments of ecstasy, they should be aware of their mortality.'

At this point, Stacey had looked up to her teacher, spell-bound by the young woman's words, and saw there, at the school mistress's shoulder, just such a black shade speaking into her ear. She'd clapped her hands and yelped with delight, appreciative of yet another educational stunt. But, instead of the consensual rapt applause that usually followed such a performance, she was met with confused glances and sniggers from the rest of her form. In fact, Stacey was then administered a sharp scolding and an instruction to pay attention.

At break time, convinced of a conspiracy, she tackled her best friend Lizzie. But, no, Lizzie had assured her, she'd seen no such spectre. Stacey was getting carried away.

The next day, in assembly, there was a disturbing announcement. With red eyes and much agitation, their headmistress sadly informed them that Ms Topping had walked out of the playground and straight under the wheels of an articulated lorry.

Bewildered and confused, Stacey rationalised the

apparition: she simply had an overactive imagination. Her mum said it, her dad had said it and her brother thought she was a fruit.

Soon a replacement teacher appeared, and Stacey almost forgot about the incident until, a month later, she witnessed the same black shade tailing an elderly neighbour across the High Street. Two days afterwards, Stacey learnt the old lady had died of a heart attack in bed that night.

Over the next few years, the apparition continued to reappear and disappear, leaving in its wake a series of corpses: Uncle Jack (missing at sea), the paper boy (car accident), cousin Nicky (stabbed in a brawl), her rabbit, Pappy (got by foxes), Bertie the budgerigar (pursued by seven swans) and many, many more.

But she was a practical girl, not prone to hysterics, and soon became accustomed to spotting Death about its duties.

However, Stacey Winters was also a compassionate soul and unable to acclimatise to the grief it left behind.

So when it came to career options she thought very carefully. There was no point going into the medical profession, she would only catch Death when it was far too late. She needed to be pre-emptive, preventative. She needed to have an authority about her that would make people listen. And thus she entered the Force.

It was a bitter lesson. Try as she might, Stacey found she couldn't outsmart Death. It was irritating and sometimes put her off her dinner. Especially when Death was hovering around the chef. And it had done precisely that, earlier this year, when she'd gone on a blind date at La Fleur restaurant.

And that poor bloke had ended up with a particularly nasty exit – on a hook, split open in the cellar. She'd had to go on duty the following day and guard the entrance to the crime scene. The whole thing made her feel guilty. Quite unsettling.

But today was different. Today was more devastating. She hated it when Death took the young.

She'd given out a loud moan this morning when, from the window of the panda car, she'd spied Daniel at the roadside, the 'Hungry and Homeless' sign on his lap and Death at his shoulder. A familiar weariness descended and, fleetingly, she was possessed by the urge to bloody well put Death in its place. Shaking her head, she'd tutted at Daniel and directed her partner, PC Gaz Maguillo, to pull over. By the time she'd got to the young beggar, the spectre had disappeared.

Daniel shivered in his soggy sleeping bag as last-minute Christmas shoppers pelted down the pavement beside him.

Stacey breathed in. The air tasted like snow was on its way.

'Daniel,' she told him, 'you need to look after yourself. Especially tonight. It's cold. Get a decent meal and a place in a hostel.'

Then she fished into her purse and hooked out a trio of twenty-pound notes. Even as she handed them over, she could sense the echo of Death around him. Yet the lad's enthusiastic reaction had been so encouraging she'd returned to the car wondering if, just maybe, perhaps *this* time she'd foil the old bastard.

And it was Christmas – the season of goodwill. Maybe Death would let her have this one as a present. Now wouldn't that be a thing?

Despite her good spirits, it really came as no surprise when, this evening, just before knocking off, they were called back to Marble Arch to size up a new corpse.

When the young constable pulled back a filthy blanket to reveal the Belsen-thin, blue-lipped Daniel, complete with needle in arm, Stacey smiled bitterly, defeated yet again.

'Overdose,' her colleague concluded. Then, pulling out a small plastic sachet filled with smack, he added, 'Looks like he came into a bit of money.'

Stacey Winters sighed. She had, indeed, put Death in his place. 'You can't outwit it,' she thought aloud.

'Come on love,' said PC Maguillo, catching the deep frown on her face. 'We're finished now. Don't know about you but I could do with a drink.'

And they had raced to the nick's social club where Sergeant Edwards was just getting into his stride.

'You'll get used to it soon enough,' the senior policeman repeated to his charge. 'You'll deal with it eventually.'

'You're right. Let's change the subject,' said Stacey, fathoming uneasiness around her. 'I can tell you most sincerely sir, I've had enough of Death today.'

'Quite right. The feeling's mutual,' Death whispered in her ear.

SHE SAW THREE SHIPS

Mr Lombardy's house was closer to St Hilliards than the cottage they had rented for their family holiday. And it was grander, with large windows that oddly did not look out on the bay below but to the south and down the coast. In fact, the unusual situation almost gave the impression the place was turning its back on the glorious view, the sun-soaked hillside and green slopes that cantered gently to the village.

Ethel-Rose thanked the driver with sincerity as she disembarked from the stylish car. She had never been in a Bentley before and hadn't expected her first time to be in Cornwall.

When she had arrived at Penrith Station she had been expecting a car. Mr Lombardy, the owner of Lillia Lodge, the cottage that her husband had hired for the family break, had previously promised collection on arrival. Which was kind. When she decided to come down a day earlier to prepare the cottage for her family, she had written to him and asked if, instead, the car might be available to pick her up then and had of course offered payment for the service. She had not received a reply but had hoped for the best.

There was, however, no one waiting. Nor were there taxis

idling. Though the station was full of bustle and voices, most of the travellers seemed to be readying for departure. No cars, she learned, were returning to the village.

If it weren't for one elderly gentleman who had been dropped off by his niece's chauffeur, she would have been stranded. Or faced a three-mile walk to Mr Lombardy's house to collect the keys. And she had her luggage and equipment to clean the house and air it before her aunt Rozalie, her husband, Septimus, and son, Teddy, arrived the following day. Her brother George had experienced problems with his lungs. Dust particularly aggravated his condition. Although there were no signs of the disease in her infant son, she was taking no chances: one could never trust the standards of hygiene in rentals. Holiday-makers were transient. Often corners were cut. But to carry her luggage for the week, her dish cloths, bleach, soaps and gloves, to carry them all the way to St Hilliards, well the thought made her sigh with despair and clutch her handkerchief to her cheek. She was strong, yes, and able of course, but three miles!

Luckily it was at this moment that the gentleman had taken her arm and guided her into the lingering Bentley.

'It was,' he said, 'no trouble at all.' His niece would understand and, Tanken, the chauffeur would be delighted to take her to Mr Lombardy's residence, then onwards if necessary to the cottage she had hired.

Tanken, however, did not look delighted at the prospect. In fact, for a moment before his mask of professionality was fastened back on, she had glimpsed a face that looked distinctly dismayed. But it had been fleeting. And in the end, because the gentleman insisted that he could not depart until 'this most fair damsel in distress' looked not so, Tanken had picked up Ethel-Rose's bags and stowed them deftly in the boot.

He was just as nifty now as he took them out and set them at Ethel-Rose's feet.

'Will that be all, Ma'am?' he asked. There was a tug on his words as he spoke, as if he were trying to expel them as quickly as possible and wanted to hear no response.

Ethel-Rose looked at the house. It had, she thought, an abandoned look to it. The blinds were down on the bedrooms of the top floor. And certainly one of the rooms with a bay window had its shutters drawn.

Last week she had briefly mentioned her concerns to her husband regarding the absence of a confirming letter. But Septimus had told her he was sure everything would be fine. Her husband was one of those types of men who always acted as if everything was fine. She had liked that about him when they first met. Back then, his reassurance had been a delicious and calming nectar. Lately though, this outlook had jarred. She desired him to be more concerned than he was. And because he wasn't, she had felt that it was up to her to work through the potential outcomes, if the cottage was unavailable. Or if Mr Lombardy was not in. She suspected if this was the case she would have to walk further into the village to find lodgings for the night. If they were available.

The uncertainty of it all was infuriating.

As a rule, she liked to plan as much as she could to keep things steady and on track. For she had come to understand that in life there were always surprises round the corner, ever ready to jump up and knock you over. And these things one simply could not prepare for. So it was up to you to do what you could. Contingency planning, she liked to call it.

She was, however, delighted, and more than a little relieved, when on ringing the bell pull, the thick front door opened and she was greeted by a young woman with dyed blonde hair and a fetching two-piece suit.

Ethel-Rose was not the only one comforted by the sight of life within.

Her driver's shoulders dropped and with a weak smile he asked, 'Ah good. Perhaps you would like me to bring your bags in, Ma'am?'

She didn't answer immediately but introduced herself to the woman, who, it turned out, was Mr Lombardy's secretary, Dorothy.

Swiftly, Tanken stowed the bags at the door under the porch.

'All right then?' he asked, awaiting dismissal.

'Yes, thank you so much. That will be all, Tanken.'

'Good luck,' said the chauffeur returning with speed to his car. 'Make sure you lock up well tonight, Ma'am. 'Tis Michaelmas Eve,' he added cryptically. 'The feast of All Angels.'

'Is that right?' asked Ethel-Rose, suitably perplexed and unsure of what the odd fellow was trying to imply.

'Aye,' he said. 'All of them.' Then he tipped his cap and was off down the gravel drive before she could ask him to explain further.

'Strange fellow,' said Ethel-Rose as Dorothy bade her to enter. 'That was an unusual farewell.'

'Oh,' said Dorothy and led Ethel-Rose into a side office. 'They're full of it down here, the locals. I wouldn't worry. Their heads are full of superstition and straw!' She beckoned to Ethel-Rose to take a chair and produced a ledger. 'So – Mrs Strange. Yes, I have you down as arriving tomorrow?'

'Ah,' said Ethel-Rose and explained about the letter.

Dorothy nodded as she followed the train of Ethel-Rose's logic. 'Yes, it all makes sense. See, Mr Lombardy is away. He goes at this time every year, I'm told. I took the position up recently, in summer. Apparently, he has a villa outside of Venice. They say the light is wonderful at this time of year.'

'How nice,' said Ethel-Rose, wondering briefly if she might ever be able to visit such exotic climes.

'Which explains the gap in communications,' Dorothy concluded. 'But it is of no matter. I have the keys here. I believe Mrs Trevelyan, the housekeeper, cleaned the lodge last week. She is planning to run over it again today. You may catch her or else I can ask her to come on the morrow.'

'Oh no,' said Ethel-Rose, thinking of dust motes spinning in the air and Ted's tiny lungs. 'Today will be just fine. I'll be glad for the company if I catch her.'

Dorothy laughed. 'Ha. You're like me!' she said and smiled. 'I'm of the same opinion.' Then a sigh escaped her. 'I do like it here. The countryside is beautiful. And this is a good position, but lonely sometimes.'

Ethel-Rose nodded. 'Yes. I can imagine. The village is not big.'

'No. We have a lot of trade in the summer but off-season the place hibernates. A lot of the residents go away. Only us poor workers have to stay.'

Ethel-Rose agreed. 'It is always the way in seaside towns. A pity for you, but a boon for us.'

'Indeed,' said Dorothy. 'It is very pleasant to see fresh faces here. And have some conversation.'

Moved by the sincerity of her smile, Ethel-Rose touched Dorothy's arm. 'Then you must come and have dinner with us at the cottage one evening this week. You will like my husband, Septimus, he is adorable, and my Aunt Rozalie is quite a character! She is gifted, you know. If you get on all right she might read your cards, tell your fortune.'

'Oh my! That would be splendid. Yes please.' Dorothy's face lit up. 'Right, I must find Mr Lombardy's man. Our Mr Trevelyan will drive you to the Lodge in the car.' And she went off.

Thirty minutes later Ethel-Rose was bumping down an old dirt track with Mr Trevelyan in a shiny blue Ford. She wondered if there was a rulebook for Cornish chauffeurs that dictated a level of sullen silence and cloudy demeanour, for Mr Trevelyan was as unforthcoming and reluctant as Tanken had been. Though she had a sense there was much he wanted to say to her. She could see it in his eyes as he picked up her bags. In that brief unguarded moment she had seen confusion become something larger and glossier, almost like fear, strong and keen as a flash of lightning and gone just as quickly.

Silence pooled in the car as they drove together over the

rocky road, and she felt herself being sucked into a feeling of despair, which was not hers. Nor was it likely to have emanated from this stony monolith of a man. It was almost as if it was coming up from the land like an unseen mist or spray. Perhaps she was simply tired from the long train journey.

Her spirits, however, were soon elevated when they turned the corner of the lane and she spied, across the tops of honey-suckled hedgerows, Lillia Lodge.

'Goodness,' exclaimed Ethel-Rose. 'It is enchanting!'

The house was one of those shingle-covered affairs that had shells pressed into mortar, and perched, like a seagull, on the uppermost ring of a crescent of mounts and bumps. It really was a handsome cottage, she could see now. The black-and-white photo in the brochure had done it no justice at all. For it was bedecked with purple wisteria and decorated with tubs of geraniums, red, white and pink. A curl of saffron-coloured roses that were growing around the door capped off such a pretty picture.

There was colour everywhere. Vivid rows of fir trees sheltered a little potting shed at its side. Even this had planters full of large violet-blue Michaelmas daisies.

Trevelyan pulled up outside the porch. Ethel-Rose got out and smiled.

She had been offered a cottage further up the bay, in St Hilliards proper, where the tangle of streets, shops, bakers, tea rooms and pubs led messily down to a white beach. 'It is more in the midst of things,' the agent had urged.

And yes, certainly it was true that Lillia Lodge stood away

from the other dwellings, up at the rockiest end of the bay. That, yes, there was no beach this end. But what the photograph had not revealed was the wonderful position of the lodge, atop the jagged crags that cradled the village.

From up here you could look down upon the whole of St Hilliards, the clusters of dwellings that spread in semi-circles around the small harbour; its boats bobbing gently in the sea; beyond them on the other side, green clifftops and grey slopes. Out on the Celtic Sea a rocky island shone in the sun.

Oh yes, this view was most certainly a fair trade for the convenience of the village.

She breathed in and smelt the sea spray, the honeysuckle, the faint tang of roses and she closed her eyes. A home from home. Sublime. This would be a charming holiday, she could tell. Just what they needed.

'No!' A voice pierced the quietness. It was coarse and loud, though female, belonging to an older person with large lungs. 'Go away. It's not ready.'

When Ethel-Rose opened her eyes she saw, there in the open doorway of Lillia Lodge, a woman in a gingham housecoat holding a dishcloth in her hand. She was shaking her head.

'No, no, no!' Fierce eyes blazed from Ethel-Rose to Mr Trevelyan. 'Not today! I told Dorothy. Take her away, Merryn.'

Above Ethel-Rose's head a seagull circled and cawed out loudly, 'No-er, no-er.'

Mr Trevelyan joined in the communal sentiment and shook his head. 'Nae Gertie. Dorothy says to bring her over.'

It did not settle the woman, Gertie, who had planted her legs firmly on the threshold and looked to be filling it up with as much of herself as possible, presenting a ferocious, fleshy barrier to anyone intent on entering within. She was between fifty and sixty years of age, with thick bones and high cheekbones, firm of body and stature and of voice.

'What does she know? Not tonight, I tell thee,' she bellowed. Her words formed a command. 'Return her to the village.'

Being spoken of in such a fashion, as if she were an unwanted item of shopping to be taken back to the store for exchange or compensation, did absolutely nothing to endear the woman to Ethel-Rose.

The incoming tenant decided to take matters into her own hands and stepped in and extended her hand to the house-keeper. 'Mrs Trevelyan, I'm Mrs Strange. It's fine. You may go. I have brought my own cleaning apparatus. Please leave the rest to me. I don't mind scrubbing. It clears my mind.'

She had reached the door and was expecting not a curtsey but at least a nod of assent.

Neither was forthcoming.

Mrs Trevelyan stayed put, as solid as a statue. But Ethel-Rose did not give up that easily and continued on her trajectory, coming face to face with a strong and high forehead. Vivid green eyes found hers and widened as they took in Ethel-Rose's face. Three blinks and then Gertie Trevelyan at last did step back. Not out of courtesy, however. Her eyes puckered in the corners then widened and distorted.

'What are you?' she asked, and gasped. For a moment a

shadow of hesitation passed over her face and she touched her stomach as if some sick feeling had twisted her bowels. But it was a brief interlude and soon the housekeeper regained herself. Glancing at her husband, Mrs Trevelyan closed the front door behind her. 'Merryn, no! This one will see. We cannot.'

But Ethel-Rose was getting tired of all this. 'Look,' she said. 'I would be awfully grateful if you admitted me and handed over the extra keys. I really am not going anywhere. It's taken me a long long time to reach Lillia Lodge and the day is nearly over. I will not find other lodgings now. Would you want me asleep on the street?'

Mrs Trevelyan stared at the young woman on the doorstep. For such a slight figure, she understood that there was formidable force in her character. It came out in her posture and bearing. And, as Mrs Strange took another step towards her, the set of her features told the housekeeper further argument would be useless. The new tenant was going to be staying in Lillia Lodge, whether she consented or not.

Mr Trevelyan must have also sensed it, for without a word he bent and picked up the cases and ferried them over to the front door. 'Let's get her settled before night comes in, eh?' he said as he met his wife on the step.

With a clear and audible sigh, which Ethel-Rose detected was more aligned to frustration than anger or indignation, Mrs Trevelyan finally stepped aside and opened the door for the young woman. 'I ain't happy about it,' she said to her husband. 'On your head be it, Merryn Trevelyan. On your head.'

Her husband lowered the offending body part and carried Mrs Strange's bags into the lodge. He set them down in a small hallway, beneath a grandfather clock that ticked loud and slow.

Ethel-Rose, who had followed him in quickly before either one of them could change their minds, headed down a narrow passage to the room at the end of the house, the kitchen, which was just then flooded with the honeyed sunshine of late afternoon. Through the windows glorious views opened up over not one but two quite lovely bays.

To the left was familiar St Hilliards, but ahead and to the right she could see there was a neighbouring bay. For Lillia Lodge was situated on a rocky pinnacle that rose up between the two crescents. The one on the right, however, contrasted immensely with St Hilliards minute harbour and fluffy sands. Over time, the cliff had fallen away into the sea, creating a sharp necklace bejewelled with great black boulders that glittered wetly around granite splinters and blade-like spikes of rock over which the ocean crashed and burst, split and roiled.

The two bays presented contrasting sides of nature – the cosy, tamed and sheltered resort on one hand. On the other a churning cauldron of wild unchecked danger – Neptune in his fury.

'But it's beautiful,' said Ethel-Rose. Something in the view, the tumult, moved her.

'Devil's Cove,' said Mr Trevelyan coming up alongside her and pointing to the darker bay. Then he shuddered.

Ethel-Rose smiled at him and moved away so he too could

enjoy the view. Absently she ran a finger over the cooker and automatically inspected her hand. Distracted thus, she noted her palm was quite quite clean. 'Oh Mrs Trevelyan!' she said, her mood once again lifting. 'You must have very high standards. I should say this room is spotless, indeed!' She laughed.

But Mrs Trevelyan, who had followed her in a lumbering fashion, did not. She went to a small wooden cabinet affixed to the wall and fished out a bundle of keys, which she threw, like a diseased thing, on the kitchen table. 'There. All the keys. You make sure you lock up tonight.'

Ethel-Rose frowned. It was ungracious she thought. But then, quite often country people lacked finesse. She knew her finishing school, which had polished her rough edges, had also scrubbed out the memories of when she too lacked subtlety. Nevertheless, at home, in Adder's Fork, they rarely locked their doors. St Hilliards did not seem, on first impression, too dissimilar. Certainly not crime-ridden. Though as she was thinking this, she remembered the tinkers who had passed through her own village but two years ago, causing havoc and mischief wherever they went. 'What? Why does everyone tell me to lock the doors?' she asked. 'Are there tinkers abroad?'

At the window Mr Trevelyan grimaced. 'Something like that.'

Ethel-Rose saw a shadow pass across Mrs Trevelyan 's face. There was no point challenging the woman, and she had no desire to enter into another battle of wills to excavate the truth. Instead, she took a breath and let her eyes roam over the kitchen, taking in the large inglenook fireplace and low beams. 'That's a wonderful fireplace there. How old is the cottage?'

Mrs Trevelyan moved, in the same lumbering way, to the feature and ran her cloth over the mantelpiece. 'Old,' she said. 'This part dates to the fifteenth century. The Watcher lived here.'

'The Watcher?'

But the housekeeper had cast her eyes to the ground. A network of thread veins flushed across her cheeks. She looked away and patted strands of her slate-coloured hair that had fallen lose from the bun at the back of her head.

Over by the windows Mr Trevelyan was fixed on something outside. She couldn't see it in detail, though it was tall and dark like a telegraph pole. Sensing her eyes upon him, the driver turned. His face was obscured, sun shining down on his back, illuminating threads of his hair and the fuzz of his vestments like a halo. He opened his arms in a strange, almost preacher-like pose so that for a moment, in that position, with just that light streaming around him, he looked like an eerie angel. 'Show her the priest-hole, Gertie. Show her,' he said to his wife.

Ethel-Rose watched Mrs Trevelyan consent, then followed as she beckoned her back into the hallway.

By the stairs the housekeeper paused and held up her large hand, directing Ethel-Rose's attention. The staircase was solid and very old, fashioned from a dark, heavy timber.

'See here,' she said, as Ethel-Rose looked on with curiosity, and she pressed against a carved mark on the wood. With a barely audible click, a door that had not been visible, swung open. It was rectangular with a triangle cut out of the side to match the incline of the stairs. Ethel-Rose was disappointed to find it concealed only a small under-stairs cupboard space that contained nothing but a carpet sweeper and a feather duster long since past its prime. 'Oh,' she said. 'I see.'

'No,' Mrs Trevelyan replied. 'Down here.' And she reached to the floor, which appeared exceedingly ordinary. 'Here,' she said again and instructed Ethel-Rose to the edge where the boards met the wall. 'A lever.' She pointed to what looked like a regular knot in the wood and put her fingers through.

To Ethel-Rose's amazement the cupboard floor popped up like a lid. Mrs Trevelyan picked it up and pushed it open. Ethel-Rose brushed her shoulder as she craned her neck and squinted into the dark void below. There was a torch hanging by a string on a nail by the duster, which Mrs Trevelyan grabbed and then shone down. The circle of light revealed a small square space perhaps only four feet high and which extended to not more than six feet in length.

'It's safe,' said a voice behind her. It made her jump. Mr Trevelyan was so close. She straightened her back but he didn't move away to give her more space. His breath touched her neck.

'Intriguing,' said Ethel-Rose, fighting against the urge to slink further back from the driver. 'Yes, I've heard of these hidey-holes.'

'This one …' he said, his eyes blazing into her. 'They say it was built by Saint Nicholas Owen, a master crafter. Dedicated his whole life to creating priest-holes to protect the clergy, give them sanctuary. He was a martyr. This here, is full of great sanctity. It was one of his last.'

'Is that so?' remarked Ethel-Rose, unsure of what was expected of her. Was she meant to stand in admiration? Bow down and pray?

She watched as Mrs Trevelyan returned the lid to its clever resting place and hoped dearly that the old couple did not intend to tour her around all of the original features in the lodge. She yawned and made sure not to disguise it. 'Thank you so much for pointing out such a charming feature. My little one will find it most amusing.'

'Little one?' The housekeeper's eyes snapped to Ethel-Rose. 'There is a child on its way? Tonight? On All Angels …?'

'No,' Ethel-Rose replied, quite alarmed by the shrill pitch of Mrs Trevelyan's voice. 'Tomorrow. That's why I have come early – to dust and clean.'

She thought the older woman was going to respond, but her husband touched her arm. 'Come on, Gertie. It is not our business.'

Mrs Trevelyan hesitated for a moment, then, much to Ethel-Rose's surprise, allowed herself to be led by her husband without a further word nor any farewell. She watched the couple trundle down the hall, out the door, over the garden and then get into the blue motorcar.

As the sound of the engine faded, she leant against the stairs and breathed out a long, sustained sigh of great relief. Now the house was hers.

It did not take Ethel-Rose long to settle herself into Lillia Lodge. There was food in the pantry and fresh milk in the new refrigerator. For supper she cooked an omelette and, after eating, washed up, made herself a cup of tea and took it rather decadently into the master bedroom, which was positioned on the first floor and was to the rear of the house. But of course, with this marvellous aspect that would have been the builder's natural choice.

There was a large window in there, which had the most spectacular view over the bays, even better than that in the kitchen. And it was here she settled herself in, with pillows and blankets and a pair of field glasses so she could sip her cup of tea and peruse the bay as the sun set.

Amber, rose and purple coloured the view as it began to sink behind the rocky island out to sea. Stars were beginning to come out in the east.

The days were shortening but the warmth had not yet drained from summer and she lazed comfortably in her little nest, looking over the two bays: by the harbour the villagers were retiring for the night, while over in the other, the waves crashed on.

She realised, as her eye roamed across the ridge and the lawns of the house, that the tall dark thing Mr Trevelyan had been staring at earlier was an old fire beacon. Though it was rusting and decrepit and could not have been used for years. She supposed it must have once functioned like some kind of lighthouse to warn seamen of the rocky dangers that awaited them if they missed the entrance of St Hilliards' harbour and blew into Devil's Cove. Those strident crags down there would surely smash a ship to pieces. *Thank goodness*, she thought, that in this modern age, they had such marvellous technologies, radar and such, secrets given up by the war. And Ordnance Surveys had come a very long way. Sailors these days were so much better positioned in terms of navigational techniques. She smiled, contented, pleased to be alive in the now, the present day, and to be there in the Lodge on such a pleasant evening.

She was not sure what woke her first – the sound or the light. It took her a few moments to realise that she must have been sleeping. For outside night had fallen. An inky blackness pooled over the sky. The moon had risen into it.

Her cup and saucer lay tilted on her lap. The last bit of tea at the bottom was cold, a cloudy residue spread over the surface. Before she could put it down on the floor, a crackling sound alerted her to activity but yards from her window seat.

The beacon, it seemed, was alight. Gassy purple flames sprouted upwards in a fluttering dance. She could not see anyone out there and wondered why she had not been informed by Mr Lombardy that the crow's nest in her rented garden might be used by strangers on occasion. She thought such an intrusion would merit an explanation or a warning. Perhaps a discount on the weekly rental. For a moment a frisson of irritation passed through her, but very quickly her attention was distracted by something gliding on the foamy breakers just out of reach of St Hilliards' piers and jetties. It was a boat, though strangely shaped. The prow curled like a Viking ship. Its mainsail rose as the wind picked up.

How lovely, thought Ethel-Rose. *Perhaps there is a pageant or flotilla tomorrow? A kind of regatta.* And she hoped that

Teddy and the family would make it down in time to see it. Though, she could see no other such extraordinary vessels.

As the boat caught the breeze, it glittered.

Perhaps there is treasure on the deck, thought Ethel-Rose excitedly. *From far off places? Exotic jewels, gold, frankincense, spices and more. Gifts for family, goods to trade. What a welcome the boat and its men would get here!*

And surely enough, as it curved into the shelter of the harbour, she saw happy little dots emerge from the houses in the village and run to greet it. The vessel docked, and cries of delight mixed with shouts of celebration carried to her on the wind. *The taverns in the village will be full of fun tonight*, she thought, and smiled.

But as she was imagining the high jinks in the hostelries below something very strange happened: the beacon in the garden extinguished itself entirely, throwing everything into darkness, as if some unseen hand had thrown ashes over it and instantly suffocated the fire. Although she squinted, she could see no moving shapes outside the house, no people or keeper, who might have done such a thing. Just the spike of the beacon, dark and alone.

At that moment the wind chose to increase its strength and the moon, which had been nearing full and shining, was obscured by turbulent clouds that had appeared from nowhere.

The gloom thickened. An eerie silence crept over the land.

As she looked down into St Hilliards' bay she saw that fingers of mist were creeping out from the harbour and blanketing the village, where she noticed all the lights had also gone out.

The Viking boat was all but obscured by the salty spray, yet above it another mast came into view, also cloaked in mist. This vessel was larger and square-rigged, its sails billowing like a giant's white handkerchiefs.

And now a tall ship, thought Ethel-Rose. Really though, in this weather it should take care and lower its sails.

She perceived the sea had become choppy – the masts tilted and twisted as the vessel ploughed through the foamy spray, which was reaching higher. Close to the shore the waves were now crested with white horses.

It's bringing in the fog, she thought and squinted. Below Lillia Lodge, she could just make out shadows moving round the cliff.

She peered down and saw that they were people, clambering over the rocks below from St Hilliards' bay to Devil's Cove.

What were they doing out at this hour on such a stormy night?

And why had they no torches?

But as they reached the further bay, she saw pinpricks of light come on. Then up the other end of Devil's Cove another beacon exploded into light.

Out in the bay, the tall ship chopped and dipped, heading it seemed, not for the shelter of St Hilliards, but the treacherous jaws of Devil's Cove.

Oh no, she thought. The crew must believe the lights were guiding them to safety, not warning them of the perils below!

She sat up, alarmed and pressed her face against the panes.

Her breath steamed up the glass. She rubbed it and saw that the lights on the beach had multiplied and were moving, to and fro, swinging back and forth as if deliberately enticing the ship in.

No, she thought. *But it will smash against the rocks!*

Then she had an idea – perhaps she should light the beacon in the garden herself?

Yes, that would be it. There might be enough time yet to warn the approaching ship.

She got to her feet, put on her shoes and raced from the bedroom down the stairs, through the passageway, out the door, round the house to the back, where she could see the beacon growing like a tree from the ground.

Oh my, it was biting out here. They said the weather in these parts was changeable but even so. Though the day had been calm she felt like now she had run into a violent tempest. The wind streamed through her hair, blowing it up and lashing her face. A bitter chill pinched at her nose and ears.

As she reached the beacon, she saw to her dismay there was no wood stacked within its metal nest. Nor cinders. Nothing. Although it had been blazing brightly just minutes ago.

Could it really have burnt itself out like that?

It was hard to think. The waves were crashing loudly now, stirring and hissing and roaring. What a storm was surely being whipped up! She blinked and searched for the bright ship out there in the thick of it, found it and gasped out loud. For the fated boat was now fast entering Devil's Cove.

'Why?' she cried, then saw stirrings below: more individuals were amassing on the craggy rim.

Thrashed by the wind, her field glasses battered about her chest. She had forgotten she was still wearing them. But now she picked them up and looked through their lenses at the folk on the beach.

Her vision rested on a woman in long skirts. That was perplexing – could Mrs Trevelyan possibly be out down there? This character had the same build and cumbersome manner of walking as the heavy housekeeper, but she was too far away to see for sure. Perhaps a relative.

Around the woman were other men. Some had scarves and jerkins fastened tight, well prepared for wind and cold. Beyond this group she saw others holding lanterns. Farm hands with scythes and pitchforks, milkmaids with their shoulder yokes and pails were descending from the other cliff. They must have come out from a nearby farm, drawn by the light and clamour, to try and aid the passengers of the vessel.

Down below, a crowd of more than thirty villagers were waving bright bundles, burning torches and lanterns, seemingly coaxing the ship towards them, urging it in.

But that could not be, for it was not a safe harbour. The vessel would be torn and ripped apart. And as she thought this, moans and cries of shock were borne aloft and over to her on the wind: the crew were becoming wise to their fate. But at last the ship was letting down its sails. A small lifeboat was lowered, swinging, into the raging waters below. Though this last ditch was too late for the men on board the larger vessel.

Borne aloft on a giant and vicious wave, propelled in a chaotic, spiralling motion by the cruel and angry sea, the ship surged forwards. It pitched and lurched.

There was a loud, grating sound, metal against metal, shattering glass, wood and timbers splintering, forced apart.

A well of cries went up from the beach as the vessel was picked up and driven forward again by the spiteful sea, piercing itself finally on the bank of rocks. Chunks were torn from the hull as it was forced, mortally wounded, into the shallows of Devil's Cove.

The torches on the beach waved furiously. A roar went up from those gathered there.

Dark little figures were jumping from the decks, abandoning ship, making for the shore.

Ethel-Rose held her field glasses to her eyes and passed them over the waves. The lifeboat was bobbing precariously. There were men in there, with oars, rowing the dingy to shore. Now it appeared the villagers had undergone a change of heart – she could hear their shouts from her clifftop, 'Here, safe harbour, here'. They were calling the lifeboat in.

Her eye caught a tiny whiteness on the scrap of beach closest to her. She shifted the binoculars and saw a man reach dry rocks on the crust of the cove.

A survivor!

And yes, she saw, he was struggling, raising his hand for help. Several villagers, the one like Mrs Trevelyan, two men who had come down the cliff with handkerchiefs about their necks, and a milkmaid, ran to the seaman, their arms outstretched.

At last, she thought. *The villagers are rallying.*

But no sooner had the beleaguered mariner been raised to his feet, a terrible thing did happen. The maid, who had been fiddling with her pail, produced a thin sharp thing, shaped like a knife. The men clutching the seaman held him up to face the women. Then the one like Mrs Trevelyan took the dagger from the maid and ran it through the seaman's heart.

Ethel-Rose cried out and dropped her glasses to the ground.

Hells Teeth! She squinted at the bay. Had she really witnessed a profane murder. What should she do?

She sank to her knees, overwhelmed by the weight of responsibility. For she concluded she must continue to bear witness to the crime and take her testimony to the police. If the local constabulary refused to act then she would hitch a lift to Truro and speak to them there. Justice for this foul deed must be meted out.

Without it, there was only chaos.

And that, also, was too much to bear.

With reluctant hands she found her glasses on the damp grass and, still kneeling, pointed them at the cove again. The murderous villagers were now gathered round the sailor's prone form. But, she saw to her disgust, they were rifling through his pockets, ripping at his clothes.

How could they degrade themselves further? This was so wrong and she hardened her resolve to fetch the authorities and judges.

When the men had picked everything from the dying mariner and the women had chewed over what was left, the four of them picked him up and cast his limp body back into the surf.

Other villagers had waded in too. For the sea had becalmed – the surface of the water was flat. The moon ventured out weakly from behind the clouds and illuminated the unfolding scene: men from the shore were clambering aboard the ship and a chain had been formed. Cargo was carefully unloaded from the hold and passed along to those waiting in the bay.

But that was stealing! That was ... and it finally dawned on Ethel-Rose that these people were not a clutter of opportunist villagers. These people were wreckers.

She had heard of them before, yet thought them just legends. Her Aunt Rozalie had read stories in which dastardly crooks used tricks, and 'false lights', to lure in sea-faring vessels so that they would run aground and be looted – they called themselves 'wreckers'. Though these here tonight were not foul criminals or gangs as depicted in the fictions, but ordinary people who worked at farms, who lived in St Hilliards, a pretty seaside town. A far cry from the depraved pirates she had imagined.

But then she had a thought – *was this why the God-fearing were deserting the place like rats from a ...?* She looked up again at the wounded ship. Did this treachery explain the crowd departing at the station? Were they leaving to avoid any part in this vile assault upon innocent men?

But then why not alert the police?

Unless the local station was in on it too?

Or perhaps they were there now? Readying to help.

She shifted the binoculars to the shore and saw that the lifeboat had reached it. The rowers were helping two women to disembark: one old and crippled, another younger but small.

The air was filled with the sounds of a pistol.

One shot, then two fired in quick succession.

Then three shots more.

Ethel-Rose had jumped at the noise and covered her eyes.

When she looked back the bodies of a man and the old woman were scattered on the sand. Around them were other corpses. Another man was struggling with his attacker. She took her field glasses away from the unfolding horror, but even without them caught the small lithe shadow of the young woman running away down the shoreline.

Two men gave chase and quickly caught up, whereupon they fell upon her.

Ethel-Rose heard shrill screams that made her heart beat so fast she feared it might rupture.

Then the men stepped away and the screams came no more.

Putting her hand to her mouth and cheek, she realised she was weeping.

A villager was returning. In his arms he carried a little body. But it was limp. She was no doctor but, even from this distance, she could tell there was no life in the poor girl.

The murderer reached what was now becoming a large pile of bodies amassing on the pebbly shore and placed his fresh victim on the top, next to the corpse of the old woman.

Someone screamed. It went on for a long long time before she realised it was coming from her own lips.

She sank even further into the ground, willing her eyes to see no more, sweat pouring from her temples.

At some point she became aware that her gaze had drifted back to the shore. There were no more passengers or seafarers there. Only bodies piled high on the beach. One of the maids was pouring liquid over the limbs and heads there, throwing it up so it touched the uppermost tangle of limbs. Another threw a torch on.

There was a sudden burst of light, then the heap of corpses that just minutes ago had been living, breathing men and women, exploded into flames.

The funeral pyre danced higher, lighting up the whole shore and the villagers standing about it, some still, heads bowed, others examining, counting their bounty.

Her stomach turned as the bitter taste of bile filled her mouth.

From out at sea she heard a strange sound and turned to search for the source. Something wispy, like a tatty flag, was moving at the end of the garden.

Could there be a ship, another one, passing into the cove? But to reach so high as to be seen over the cliff? Well, it must be huge. Was it indeed possible, for something so large to get so close to shore?

The distinct and deafening chime of a bell spread out over the land and into the cove. She put her hands to her ears, understanding at once that whatever made it must be giant-like, to resonate with such strength. It came again – a deep melancholy knell, echoing into Devil's Cove. The people there stopped their activity and faced the sea.

Ethel-Rose followed suit and turned her field glasses out, spluttering as the noxious smell of burning flesh reached her and filled her nostrils.

The ship was sailing into the cove.

But, indeed, this one was far bigger than that which had run aground. This had four masts, and sails that, strangely, appeared ... looked ... she faltered. 'Infirm' was the only word she could find to describe what she saw. And as she took in the foggy, wavering outline glistening before her, every single drop of blood in her body seemed to freeze.

Adorned with pearls of mist, formed from undulating shadow, the ship slipped closer. Her eyes ran over the beams, the raggedy sails trailing gossamer threads, which hung down, empty of wind. Yet it was moving at a good speed.

But no, it too was heading for the shipwreck! If it wasn't careful it would suffer the same fate.

Driven by moral compulsion Ethel-Rose got to her feet and waved the field glasses.

'Weigh anchor,' she shouted at it. 'No further. There are wreckers,' she yelled.

But it had no effect. The ship continued towards her over the rocks.

Over the rocks!

How could that be? She stood stock still.

But boats needed water to move. This must be an illusion: shadows in the swirls of mist and fog.

She pressed her top lids down then, slowly, first left, then right, opened her eyes again.

But there it was – bold and solid yet simultaneously shifting, dissolving and reappearing, a miraculous mirage on the shore.

Where it stopped.

Another ear-splitting peal rang out from the prow across the sands.

The chain gang had ceased its activity and the men were staring into the mist. At the spectral ship.

And there, up on the deck, there was movement.

Rope ladders were being thrown down. Over the sides of the boat pale forms flitted, and she saw them beginning to descend.

Behind it the funeral pyre danced higher, deepening the shadows to this side. Yet she could still make out some of the villagers – who were beginning to turn away. She shifted her gaze to the bottom of the ship where the sailors were disembarking, shambling across the craggy coast.

Yet, they didn't look like ordinary seamen.

They were dark and slight.

She held up the field glasses and focused them on one of the sailors at the fore.

His dress was old-fashioned. He wore a frayed jacket and dusty tricorne hat, the like of which she had seen sailors wear in pantomimes. She only glimpsed his face, yet in that brief moment she had the impression the poor man was gruesomely disfigured.

Everything was happening so quickly.

She saw the mariner unfasten his belt and bring out a scabbard. In a jerking, almost mechanical action, white fingers handled the belt and she watched him unsheathe a cutlass. The light of the pyre glinted on the blade.

Ethel-Rose took a step back as the sailor began to approach the gathered crowd. Swiftly, without pause, he reached them. Holding the cutlass above his head she saw a glimmer of a smile cross his lips. Then he brought the weapon down across the heads of three villagers. One went down, the others began to turn but the ghastly mariner was fast upon them, the cutlass whipping up and down with frightful speed.

Cries of panic rose into the air, carried to Ethel-Rose on her cliff. She gulped in and blanched, knowing, through some black intuition, what was coming.

And surely enough, a tall grim sailor jumped from the boat, then another, with more from the ladders following their lead. In their hands all waved weapons: knives, swords and daggers, which they thrust stiffly through the villagers' bodies time and time again.

She could see a couple trying to flee, making their way to the cliff that led up to Lillia Lodge.

To her.

And though she wanted to tear her eyes away from the slaughter she found she could not move. Her body was forcing her to bear witness to this most unholy of acts.

A scuttling alerted her to an approach. Soil, pebbles and stones were falling at the garden's edge where the lawn gave way to the cliff.

Dropping the binoculars, she stared and saw a hand reach

up and clamp on to the lawn, clawing its way like a fork on the grass. A man, who resembled Merryn Trevelyan, climbed up into the garden. He did not seem to see her and once he had scrambled upright he moved swiftly across the garden into the shadows of the house.

A couple of seconds passed before yet more scuffing sounds returned her gaze to the cliff edge. One of the seamen was following on. A tricorne appeared, rising up over the cliff edge, followed by a body moving in a strange, jolting way.

Every single hair on her body rose up.

For where the seaman's face should have been there was only a skull. Where the eyes should have been, a queer darkness glowed. Beneath them she glimpsed a hole for a nose, yellow bones of the neck, the fractured collarbone tattered with scraps of old skin, beginnings of a lumpy ribcage. A creature drawn from nightmares.

Fear began its full descent.

On her knees she tried to push back and away from the advancing spectre. But her limbs were not easy to move. It was as if she had been pinned, yet not quite paralysed, by the horrendous sight.

As the atrocious phantasm emerged fully onto the grass, its skinless jaw dropped open, suspended only by threadlike sinews. A strange groan came out of it – an enormously deep, cavernous moan that combined both despair and savage fury.

It bowled into Ethel-Rose, levelling her with a sense of horror, dismay, indignation, rage, brutality, violence. She could feel the thing's most bitter madness stretch its tendrils round her neck and paw at the edges of her soul.

The avalanche of feeling, of dread, of terror, that this unleashed, however, did not overwhelm Ethel-Rose but, contrarily, sharpened her senses, and, in that very moment, as the sailor's grief washed over her she understood what the spectral crew had come for.

Of course, she thought, *it must be so.*

Retribution and punishment. Yes, indeed. The scales of justice must be tipped into balance by the sacrifice, the execution, of the villagers. Those that did not flee on Angels' Night. Those left behind. And she drew breath, wondering how they chose, but as she did she realised the creature had brought an odour up with him – not, now, burning flesh. It was something more akin to rotting, dampness and decay. It made her retch and she clutched her chest wanting to bend over, to vomit, to expel the awful smell, the feelings of treachery that were invading her very heart. But the thing was raising its hand. And in its bony grip she saw the cutlass.

It does not know I am not of their blood, she realised as it began to stalk towards her. But it could not have her. She had done no wrong and she had a son and a husband who needed her. The thought of her family, bereft and alone, spurred an energy within and she reared up and turned and began to run for the safety of the lodge.

Once inside the cottage she closed the front door and, panting, pulled the bolts across. Tearing into the kitchen, she could see, through the windows, a steady stream of ghostly mariners filing across the lawn. Though they stumbled, and some collapsed, their tawdry remains coming apart, she knew the crew would not stop until they had achieved their aim. They would be relentless.

Something heavy rapped three times on the front door.

Ethel-Rose turned and looked down the hallway. Outside, the creature was battering against the wood. If all the spectres followed him it surely would not be long till the door gave way and they would fall upon her.

She needed to find a safe space. Somewhere to hide from the diabolical crew.

Sanctuary.

Then she remembered it – the priest-hole beneath the stairs.

Yes, there!

As the lost souls congregated at the porch, piling high against the door, and the clamours for blood filled her head, she calmed herself: the priest-hole was a place of sanctity, created by a saint. It would, if anything could, provide a safe haven.

Taking in deep breaths she moved her fingers over the wood until she felt the edge of a lever.

The door sprang open and, as it did, she heard the clattering of bones across the slate tiles.

The avenging spectres were inside the house.

Quickly, on the floor, she felt around for the next door. Moans filled the passage. A coldness was flowing through the house, bringing mist and chill.

At last the lid sprang open. She flung herself into the void, knocking her head. Just as she drew the lid shut something heavy and brittle banged hard against it.

In the darkness she closed her eyes, jammed a fist into her mouth and rocked herself back and forth.

Above her the scratching began.

The light blinked with dazzling force into her hiding place.

She didn't know how long she had been down in the priest-hole. It could have been days.

Unused to the brightness she shielded her eyes and tried to make out the shadow above her.

'You've come through,' said Mrs Trevelyan. The older woman extended her arm. 'Take it.'

Ethel-Rose complied and let herself be pulled up.

The housekeeper looked her over then, as if satisfied by what she found, took her by the shoulders and pushed her into the kitchen where she sat her down.

Mrs Trevelyan sighed. 'There ain't no bother a cup of tea can't fix.' Then she went to light the stove.

The sun was shining, filling up every corner of the room with wholesome brightness, glittering on the turquoise sea outside. As she looked, dazedly, out of the window, Ethel-Rose could see no evidence of the ships of the night, the fallen villagers and ghastly crew. But then, somehow, she had come to know this would be the case.

'I saw three ships,' she said simply.

'Yes,' said Mrs Trevelyan. The kettle began to scream. 'Every year on the feast of All Angels.'

'Angels,' repeated Ethel-Rose. 'But heavenly beings ... those were no heavenly beings,' she protested.

Mrs Trevelyan placed the teapot on the table. 'Not all

of them are good. Michael fought against Lucifer, and remember the prince of darkness once had wings too. The Feast of All Angels is when we pay the price for our ancestral crimes. The sins of the father shall be visited on the child ...' And she broke off and looked away.

In profile Ethel-Rose could see that the housekeeper did bear a great resemblance to the woman she had seen on the beach. 'Was it you there that I saw?' she asked.

Mrs Trevelyan shook her head. 'Not me but a hotch-potch of family gone back, years, decades, centuries past. Who knows? I don't. Though I feel it each time – the blade through the heart.'

'But, how can it be?' she said, though she knew such things came to pass.

'People like you wouldn't understand,' said the house-keeper, and shook her head.

Ethel-Rose nodded. 'Actually, people like me fully understand.'

'Not seers,' said the housekeeper with contempt. 'Outsiders.'

'Oh,' said Ethel-Rose, aware that this was an odd and flatly honest conversation she was having.

'Now,' said Mrs Trevelyan, brusque again and workman-like. 'We don't talk about this sort of thing and neither should you. Was a nightmare that you won't have again. And you'll forget it. By noon the memory will have dimmed and all you'll be left with is an uncomforting itch. Don't let it spoil your holiday. Now perhaps you'll take advice and not come back at the same time again.'

'No,' said Ethel-Rose. 'I might stay put next year.' Suddenly Essex, with its witches and assortment of oddities, seemed the most wonderful place in the world.

MADNESS IN A CORUÑA

As dictated to Samuel Stone, curator
of the Essex Witch Museum

Halloween is the worst time for it.

You ask me why?

Walking the streets is one thing. I find myself alert to slipping ghouls, dark-backed creatures, shadows unpeeling from crevices and walls. The taint of real horror that swarms in with them is real and profound.

Holiday fun, they say.

Not so for me.

It brings it all back.

Sometimes on those nights I must look behind, double lock my doors, light incense and thank God for friends and American travellers.

Yes, even me.

And you want to know why.

Well, your instincts are right. Doctor Bradley said you were smart. Though I doubt you will find any explanation in your books at the Witch Museum. Not for this. No. Though perhaps the old man will understand. Mr Strange, I hear, has led an interesting life.

All right then.

I don't really want to mention how I came to be in A Coruña but I suppose it has some relevance to the story and you will desire to hear of it I expect, so I may as well get it over with.

I had recently divorced. There. Judge me if you will. It is the least of it.

Sheila, my former wife, was twenty-five years my junior and a student at Litchenfield University where, as you know, I lectured in semiotics. Before you leap to conclusions, she had not taken my course. Oh no, Sheila read Modern English, my colleague's department – the much-feted popinjay and television celebrity, Professor George Chin. He was so much more 'relatable' apparently and certainly more glamorous than my humble self.

It was at Chin's exclusive Christmas gathering, huddled round his minimalist wood burner, that I happened upon my future wife. If perhaps she had taken my own course, then she may have understood more of my character and our marital trundle towards collapse would have proved less arduous. As it was, we worked our way through several Relate counsellors and two tedious and expensive psychotherapists before reaching the mutual conclusion that happiness was not to be found in each other. Privately I had discovered this for myself a couple of months into the marriage: Sheila was lean and pretty, but shallow and materialistic in a way that I found distasteful. The revelation wilted my ardour.

My young wife, never the pragmatist, insisted on trying to save our doomed union. Or more likely she thought she might save me.

THE TWELVE STRANGE DAYS OF CHRISTMAS

There was a reason, as there always is, that I had remained a bachelor into my forties, yet she was determined to ignore it. Perhaps I presented a challenge to her. I don't know.

However, as the months passed and Sheila came to know me more, she began, also, to formulate the point of view that I was less aesthetic than aesthete. Women whom I have met and seduced in the past often assumed that when I am thinking, or abstracted, I am contemplating the depths of life (or them). Whereas I am simply vacant or considering the semiotic deconstruction of whatever advertisement, signage or symbol lies within eyesight.

At the beginning of our courtship Sheila would regularly catch me in this reflection and ask what I was thinking about. And so, in the early days, anxious to hang on to the fragile relationship and the exciting nocturnal theatrics it brought, I would tell her I was gauging the exact shade of her eyes, or the palette of her hair as the sun played upon it so I could burn them into my soul. I expected her to laugh, but she didn't. She purred and was more appreciative in bed. I could have done more but I have never been partial to histrionics. Remember that, please.

Once Sheila and I had been joined in matrimony I thought it wise to be honest and, anyway, I was growing bored of her persistence and vanity. So when my wife would repeat her question concerning my mental attentions, I began to tell her the truth. Disappointment would cloud her eyes for a second, before she could recycle it into an outward show of interest. Though by our six-month anniversary her mounting dismay was harder to conceal. Soon after she stopped asking.

It was with relief not bitterness that I bade Sheila farewell. One warm spring day, I watched her jump into the car of her new lover, an art student of her own age, within whom she found, or thought she had found, qualities lacking in my good self. I wished her luck sincerely, though I doubt she believed me. I have never been an emphatic man.

When term ended, unencumbered by a wife, I found myself at liberty to wander wherever I pleased. And it pleased me to go to A Coruña where I might reacquaint myself with an old university friend. Xosé was a very decent chap who I had shared a flat with briefly at Cambridge.

It had been years since I had seen him. He had married Tatiana, an elegant, black-haired Spanish beauty, and produced two similarly blessed children. They had been unable to make our wedding, though I wondered if they had simply refused to bear witness to my undoubted humiliation. And perhaps that is why, out of everyone, I chose to visit them.

My first night in A Coruña was delightful. I caught up with Xosé in a tapas bar on what he informed me the locals called Calle Vino, 'Wine Alley'. One of the children was sick and Tatiana had opted to stay in. But she sent her love and had instructed Xosé to introduce me to the local speciality, *pulpo*, boiled octopus, and to consume vast quantities of Galician wine and beer. He made a sterling effort.

Though I did not reveal it, the pulpo I could not get on with. I found the look of the dish aesthetically displeasing: swaddled in red sauce as if it were still bleeding, the bubbled skin was a rusty vermilion in shade. Purple shadows clustered round the suckers, like scorched bruises and septic sores.

However, I surrendered eventually to Xosé's inducements to sample the 'pride of Galicia' and popped a braised tentacle into my mouth. As I chewed it I could have sworn I felt it move in my mouth. Only impeccable manners prevented me from spitting the thing onto the table. With great difficulty I swallowed. But I couldn't shift the notion that later the amputated limb would swim in my stomach, feeling for ways to get out.

Instead I favoured the wine, which was, thank goodness, excellent.

We drank non-stop, exchanged stories and news and, at leisure, Xosé pointed me to several A Coruña attractions I should ensure I saw. This week, he informed me with enthusiasm, was the perfect time to experience the city, for their famous fiesta had begun. Musical performances and parades were taking place in the squares and piazzas and, on Saturday, there was to be a special concert on the beach. Madness, the English ska band of great repute, were to play he told me with a wink, and reminded me of one of my more exuberant moments at our Student Union many, many years ago. I had finally given in to his demands to dance to one of their hit records and made a happy fool of myself in front of a gaggle of undergraduates. I rarely let my guard down and was known for my reserve. The incident had ended up in the rag mag and, for a moment in time, I was to appreciate a small measure of notoriety. I had forgotten about the episode entirely and, teased into laughter by my Spanish friend, found myself briefly dosed with optimism. Xosé, too, bolstered by wine and warmth, grew loquacious and went on to recall one of our other capers – a nocturnal dip in the baroque fountain situated in the city square – fully clad and fully inebriated. He clapped me on the back and told me that night had sealed our friendship. But his recollection was flawed, for that was not me but another fellow, limp, pale and effeminate, whom I had secretly loathed.

I did not correct Xosé.

Nor did I smile.

The evening was shortened by an unexpected power cut, which seemed to provoke much consternation in the locals. I was keen to continue but, despite power returning within minutes, the bars shut and Xosé informed me he should check on his family. However, the occasion had proven so pleasant that we agreed to do it again and meet same time, same bar the following evening. Xosé promised he would see if they could get a babysitter so he could bring Tatiana along.

My hotel room was perfectly adequate but uninspiring: the view took in an empty apartment building built during the housing bubble and abandoned once it had burst. So the next morning I breakfasted and got out into A Coruña as soon as I could.

The hotel was situated right on the avenida, or promenade, as I kept calling it. A curving stone balustrade had been built at some point in the last two centuries to prevent people falling off the walk onto the rocky beach some fifty feet below. Being an Englishman abroad I felt it only polite to sample the waters and take myself for a morning dip.

Seagulls squawked and dove in circles just above me as I descended the seventy stone steps to the beach. I found a patch of silver sand near the steep rocks that curled either side of the bay and disrobed somewhat self-consciously. The Spanish families paid me no attention as I entered the sea. I was an unremarkable middle-aged man, set apart only by the radiating whiteness of my skin and lack of muscle definition. I have never been a gym man.

The sea was part of the Atlantic and, I found, sixty shades of shivering blue. Undeterred by the icy quality I took the plunge, literally, and, once the shock had passed through my limbs, swam out into the deeps. A Coruña was luminous and, despite the cold, I found myself relaxing into what Sheila would have called 'holiday mode'.

The rust-coloured cliff on my left was peppered with bathers on towels and a couple of statues – a mermaid in green and some kind of religious character I couldn't make out. Above them the promenade pushed its cafés and bars forward for custom. The streetlights, I noticed, were shaped like crucifixes, their lights fixed either side of the cross. They pointed firmly out to sea, forming a linear barrier to any unholy visitors who might consider sailing in. Or perhaps, I considered later, to keep them in.

After fifteen minutes or so I had had enough and turned inland, propelling myself back with a leisurely breaststroke.

It took me a while to notice the man on the balustrade. I had been enjoying the view of two pleasantly shaped young ladies playing bat and ball and was disappointed when the taller brunette missed (I had backed her for a winner). Her attention had been caught by something high up. Her

SYD MOORE

partner shouted out some rebuke but when the brunette did
not reply she too followed her friend's gaze, as did I.

Standing on top of, not behind, the stone balustrade was a
young man, casually dressed in shorts and T-shirt. It was clear
that he was in some distress. He was shouting, but not at
anyone in particular. His face pointed up to the sky, at which
he threw up a fist before slapping hard at the right side of his
neck. Some others on the beach, those not prone on towels
but who had been standing or walking or engaged in some
other activity had also become aware of the man and a ripple
of foreboding spread in waves through them. I felt it too as I
looked up, and increased my speed to the shore.

On the promenade a cluster of people had formed around
him, and I wondered suddenly if this was a performance
scheduled as part of the fiesta. The reaction on the beach
suggested if this was the case it was certainly not appreciated.
An old couple by the rocks shook their heads, and I saw the
life guard, who had been lazing in a deck chair, set off at
speed towards the stone staircase.

As I got closer I could see that some of the families had
called in their children and were huddling together unsure
of what to do.

The young man seemed not to notice the crowd around
him and continued his strange routine, yelling to the heavens
then again striking hard at his neck until, as I looked on, he
rather suddenly stopped. His hands dropped to his sides,
and his body became slack, as if he were surrendering to
something or someone. Then, as we all looked on, he spread
his arms out in a Christ-like pose. I saw his mouth open and

shut but was too far away to hear what he said. I think he closed his eyes, I'm not sure, but something happened, some small gesture that spoke to the audience before him, and I, like them, at once realised what he was going to do. In the next instant, before anyone could galvanise themselves into action, the young man took a step off the balustrade.

His fall was not flailing. There were no signs of regret as he pitched forwards and landed with a loud crack on the rocks below.

At first no one moved or spoke. It was as if collective shock had paralysed the entire community of witnesses. Then someone screamed and the beach fell apart into hysteria. Too late we heard the police siren approach.

I came up onto the shore and grabbed my towel. Although I tried to avoid it I could see the bloody mess where the boy's head had been. He hadn't survived the fall.

Taking my cue from the families fleeing, I clambered over the boulders to the right and made my way over another beach then up a different flight of steps.

The police had begun cordoning off the area, which included my hotel. Traffic was snaring up around me, drivers honking their horns, pedestrians gathering for a peek at the body.

I hurriedly put on my clothes and, not really knowing what to do, slipped off the main drag and into a tiny side street.

The experience of witnessing the suicide had upset me. No, not upset me. Perhaps unbalanced my mind for a moment. I am not given to sentimentality and realise that life, with its woes, is not for everyone. After Sheila's departure, despite my relief, I can admit that I experienced some dark thoughts. I firmly believed men and women should have the right to end life, if it is their own, as much as they have to create it. Not everyone was suited to twenty-first-century living. However, I was aware I had witnessed a violent tragedy that would affect many people. Not just the young man and his family but everyone who had been on the beach.

Briefly I wondered why the fellow had chosen such a public spot. But when people reach that state, rationality has already evaporated. I knew that. It was not worth thinking on. Instead, I realised, I should shirk off my growing unease by way of self-medication. I entered the first bar I came across.

There were others in there who had witnessed the suicide and when I explained to the woman I wanted a whisky, she eyed my wet shorts and beach towel with sympathy and fetched a large shot at once.

I took my drink out onto the terrace and tried to immerse myself in the sights of the street. Men who had been on the promenade were clustered around the bar, only a few feet behind me, and I could hear what they were saying. My Spanish is not good, but I caught a few phrases. I gathered the young man believed he was being pursued. By whom or what I could not translate. They were referring to the incident as an accident, though I was sure it had been premeditated to some extent. The word 'volver' cropped up a lot. One rare occasion when I accompanied Sheila to the cinema we watched an Almodóvar film of the same title, so I understood the word meant 'to return'. The young man had apparently been shouting it earlier, as a warning. He thought that someone was coming back to A Coruña. Why this should terrify him to the point of self-annihilation was beyond me. The talk and speculation became wilder and less coherent. My poor grasp of the language and inability to follow began to irk so I made off back to the promenade.

Police tape clung about the street lights and balustrade and wound itself around the front of my hotel. No one was allowed entry. Luckily I had had the foresight to bring my day pack, which contained my wallet, a t-shirt, some water and a map of the town. I would need them all now. I turned and made my way through the narrow warren of streets. Named affectionately by the locals as 'the neck', it links the round land mass at the north (the head), to the greater part of the mainland (the shoulders).

At some point during my stay I had intended to visit the city's unique lighthouse, reputed to be the oldest in the world. Unable to return to the hotel, I decided that now would be as good a time as any.

Set high upon a rocky outcrop, the *Torre de Hércules* was built in the first century by the Romans, who labelled this part of Spain *Finis Terrae* – the end of the world. Looking out into the grey Atlantic that stretched to seeming infinity, I could see why they had named it so. This part of A Coruña had a peculiar atmosphere to it. Or perhaps it was that the sun had clouded over, dimming the light, and my spirits had not yet recovered from the shock of the morning. The landscape felt besieged and anxious. Tense. Like it was waiting for something to happen.

After queuing for twenty minutes I was let into the monument. Navigating around the foundations I learned the tower got its name from a local legend. Early on in its life the town had been plagued by Geryon, a strange vindictive creature said to be the grandson of Medusa. Often described as a monster, or a shade with human faces, he was immortal, pale as snow and uncomfortable in the light, yet born with the ability to grow wings at will and fly.

Understandably the natives were rather upset with him setting up locally and feasting on the blood of the young peasant population, whom he would infect with a lunacy that led them either into the pit of insanity or compelled them to become his followers and slaves. But what could they do? Geryon was immortal.

Eventually their prayers were answered when Hercules arrived in town. The hero battled Geryon for three days and three nights before finally killing him by cutting off his head. Hercules decreed that Geryon's head must be buried deep in the ground and a tower should be built on top of it that should always burn with bright light to prevent the monster reforming and returning to wreak his vengeance.

A good story. No doubt the colourful myth put the lighthouse on the Roman map.

I made my way up five levels, noticing as I counted the steps up, that there were five on each turning. At the top, I looked up to see a magnificent rotunda fashioned from golden stone and noted, wryly, there was no light burning.

The view from the top was indeed breathtaking. One could see for miles across the Costa da Morte, the 'Coast of Death', so named because of its numerous shipwrecks. I could have stayed for longer, but the platform was filling up with cantankerous tourists, and although my mood had been lifted by the sights afforded from this vantage point, anxiety now seemed to be drifting back.

I exited hurriedly, keen to escape the crowds and walked, at a pace, down the causeway. At the bottom an old man in tattered clothing, wearing very large, black-rimmed spectacles, was standing on a soap box. Around him were several placards scrawled with slogans. I paused, curiosity overcoming my keen desire to leave, and screwed my face to the signs. It was useless, the man's handwriting was impossible to decipher. I began to move on, but he shouted at me. I stopped politely and, unable to communicate verbally, nodded and smiled. The man grimaced, then waved my attention to the tower and barked out a string of hard-lettered words. Beside him was a picture of the Tower with a cross beneath it. He grabbed it and held it to me. He was clearly insane: I smiled with as much sympathy as I could muster, then firmly turned my back on him, unheeding of his loud protestations, and made my way quickly to the road.

I now had a choice. To go back and see if the hotel was accessible or to continue to explore and stay out until it was time to meet Xosé and Tatiana. I saw from the map that I was near the old part of the city. I would regret not visiting it, if this turned out to be my only opportunity. And realistically I had been gone only three or four hours. The likelihood was that the police investigation and subsequent clear-up was still ongoing. Decision made, I wound my way through the old city wall into the most ancient part of A Coruña.

Traipsing up and down the narrow alleys I admired the baroque architecture of the churches, the tiled floors, wrought-iron decorative features, and enclosed glass balconies and *galerías*. The afternoon heat seemed to be building, reflecting off the ancient painted houses with their glorious lemon, honey and peach exteriors. I was sweating profusely and, finding myself hungry, located a café that had not closed for siesta. I selected a table on the terrace shaded by a voluptuous vine-covered pergola complete with hanging grapes. It was while I was waiting for the dreadlocked waitress to notice me that my eyes roamed over the local graffiti. Several walls were decorated with stars, formed of five points. On the floors by the gutters I identified triangles with circles drawn within. Some of these had a 'handle' or tag written beneath them, 'M.A.L' or mal. I enjoyed graffiti – it gave me something to occupy my mind on various travels – but I had no respect for the fashion of tagging, which seemed to represent nothing more creative than a canine-like inclination to mark out territory. It occurred to me that I had seen both these symbols throughout A Coruña. I was prepared to put them down to a fashion or fad, when I remembered the five floors of the lighthouse. The stars could be pentagrams, an ancient symbol of protection, though a rather pagan practice for a Catholic city. Galicia, it was true, was proud of its pagan heritage, which Xosé had told me was Celtic. The circle within the triangle however, I thought, had a Hermetic origin. Probably, I reflected, it was the totem of a local pop band, spread throughout the city in some kind of obtuse marketing campaign. I had observed such nonsense before.

I ate a fine meal of tapas, marinated mussels and Russian salad, noting a curious architectural feature in the streets around the café. The ground floor windows of each house or shop were crossed heavily by iron bars. The place seemed so harmonious and full of old world courtesy, that I wondered what the Coruñians might be protecting themselves from in such a blanket fashion. Could it be each other?

When I commented on this the waitress rolled her heavily mascaraed eyes and shrugged, dismissing me with a word: '*maligno*'. Something had been lost in translation. Was she referring to the name of the band, or the graffiti artist? I sighed and tried to string a clearer sentence together. An older man, maybe the owner, called across from behind the till, '*No preguntes*'. I smiled, again unable to comprehend his meaning and decided to nod back acquiescently. I'm glad I did, for later I learned he was instructing me not to ask questions.

I made my way east through the sloping streets, eyes fixed on the uneven roads until I reached the harbour when, aware of both the heat and my lack of hydration, I stopped for a beer in a small jazz bar off the main square, *Plaza de Maria Pita*. From there I wound my way until I came upon a curious island. Having left both my watch and mobile in the hotel I had no idea of the time, but I was keen to view the small castellation that occupied the islet, though Xosé and Tatiana had not recommended it. I walked up to the short rampart, noticing in the car park outside a number of camper vans and caravans. Xosé had mentioned it was a tradition of some Spaniards to tour the region in such a way. I thought it odd as there were no facilities here by way of toilets or showers.

It became clear that the hour was late: the cashier was counting the till and there were few other tourists about. Regardless of this I went into the castle.

It was, I learnt from the few sections of English signage, the *Castillo de San Antón* and dated back to ancient times. Certain areas were thought to be prehistoric. At one point it had been a leper colony attached to the main town by the thread of road. For the most part it served as a fort for the defence of the A Coruña harbour but it had also been a prison until the 1960s. I saw how the casements in the central courtyard could easily be converted into cells with a metal grid. These now housed stone artefacts: coffins, coats of arms, fallen gargoyles. Some stone slabs had strange ethereal creatures etched onto them, thin and colourless with long fingers and slits for eyes, their heads surrounded by tulip-shaped halos though they didn't look the least bit holy. There was no information to tell me who they were so I moved on.

The fort was oddly shaped, with a jagged star-like structure that came off a wide 'stem' – the battlements and sentry points. On the top floor were a couple of exhibitions. One of baroque furniture, another chronicled the Peninsular War. I lingered in the chapel and noticed along the wall a line drawing, which depicted a winged beast with the face of a man, the paws of a lion, the body of a wyvern and a poisonous sting at the tip of his tail. A spark of recognition flared now I was seeing the full body and I remembered the character – it was Geryon again. Not only had he provided the head under the lighthouse, it was also Geryon, I now recalled, who roamed the dark depths of Dante's *Inferno* below the seventh and eight circles of Hell, those of violence and fraud. There were more pictures to view but the atmosphere inside was becoming stifling. I went outside and found, up some stairs, a terrace. At the top I was able to see another little lighthouse on the uppermost section of the star. It was tiny, dwarfed by its older sister on the other side of the 'neck'. But unlike the other, this one was much neglected and covered in dust and ivy. I made my way over and circled it till I came upon a small wooden window. I don't know what compelled me to look in, I doubt I ever will. I suppose perhaps I was curious. I deeply wish I hadn't, for as I pressed my nose up against the glass a hideous face within rose up to view me. I had only a fleeting impression of it before instinct kicked in and I snapped my neck back.

What I saw will stay with me for the rest of my life, however long that may be.

The head was malformed, almost triangular in shape. The skin colour, if it was indeed skin, for it was glistening and cadaverous and seemingly formed of scales, was a kind of blue-grey. The hair hung down thinly, a leached-out colour of mould or dank moss.

But its eyes were the most upsetting aspect – a clotted blood-red, large black pupils that not only saw me in that brief moment of contact but looked deep inside my soul and recognised it. I felt a deep knife of fear slice me. Fortunately, at that point adrenaline flooded my senses, impelling me out of there, and I took off as quickly as my legs could take me.

Momentarily overwhelmed, however, I took a new route, one that I had not taken on my way in and, instead of arriving at the exit tunnel, I came into a dark section I had not been in before, a part of the castle that was prehistoric, which formed the cistern of the place. The cavern was coloured in the most garish colours – florid mauve and emerald slicks adorned the wet walls. The walkway came out onto a small platform that looked across a deep, deep pool of water, which had found its way up from the network of caves and tunnels stretching far below the foundations of A Coruña. I stopped for a moment, panting, and grabbed hold of the steel bars that extended across the platform to stop the foolhardy falling in. Just as I did, I felt a sharp stabbing pain on the right side of my neck. My hair fluttered as if wind had displaced it and I heard the rustle of wings by my shoulder. I spun round just in time to see a bat-like shadow fly up and into the dark of the underground cavity. Putting my hand to my neck I saw, as it came away, that it was speckled with blood.

Yes blood!

It was enough.

I turned on my heel and ran and ran and ran until finally I crossed the dark courtyard into the exit, stopping only when I was firmly out of its jurisdiction and in the safety of twilight.

I must have looked a sorry state as I leant against the metal posts outside the *Castillo,* trying desperately to calm my breath, for soon I became aware of a voice behind me.

'Hey buddy. Buddy, are you okay?'

It came from a man about my age, with long hair and a beard. Hank, I learned, was touring Spain in a campervan. 'When in Rome …' he said with a shrug as he led me into his modest dwelling to put antiseptic on what he diagnosed as an animal bite.

'Let's hope old Geryon hasn't been out and about again,' he said with a chuckle. But his words frightened me.

'Why do you say that?' I snapped angrily. I was annoyed and rather ashamed of myself for allowing fear to take hold.

Hank barely reacted to my brusque behaviour. I would come to learn the man was unflappable and I would be grateful for that later. 'Oh it's just a legend. Didn't you read about it in there? The last time this was a prison there was a massacre. The prisoners got out and killed each other. When they found the bodies all their blood was drained out. The townsfolk put it down to Geryon.'

But he's dead and under the tower, I wanted to say, shocking myself with such an irrational train of thought. Instead I said, 'Old continental superstition no doubt.'

'Uh huh,' said Hank and applied a plaster to my neck.

'I'm not surprised their imaginations run wild with that deformed lighthouse keeper,' I suggested, recalling the wretched face at the window.

'Don't think so, buddy,' Hank said. His eyebrows had risen significantly. 'That one's not been working for years.'

He was wrong of course. I had seen him. But I was not one to quarrel with my host. Instead I said, 'Geryon!' and tittered. 'Peasant stories.'

'Just because it's a story,' Hank replied in a low voice, 'doesn't mean it's not true.'

The man was clearly not on the same wavelength as me.

I thanked him sincerely for his help and explained I would be joining friends shortly for a drink and told him the name of the bar should he want to join us. It seemed the least I could do.

He shrugged and lit a suspicious-smelling rolled cigarette, telling me he might 'swing by later'. A generous host, he offered me a tug on the joint. I took it and breathed in a heady lungful of cannabis. It did me no good for almost immediately I began to feel disorientated and dizzy.

It was almost the hour to meet Xosé and Tatiana. I took my leave and began to walk back through the harbour. But as I did a strange sense reared up over me, the feeling that I was being followed. And I wondered if perhaps the lighthouse keeper desired to speak to me. I shuddered at the thought of seeing that face again. Though I cast several glances over my shoulder, as I made my way along the piazza, I could see no one following me.

As I progressed, the feeling grew to such a degree that I started to jog along the pavement. Despite becoming breathless I was reluctant to stop, and began to notice on the streets a number of misshapen people: women with bulbous eyes and cheeks coloured in purplish bruised skin with sores round their mouths like octopus suckers. Men, white and sickly bumped into me, gazing with what I imagined was malignant intent.

I passed a temporary stage erected for the fiesta and saw

on there a traditional troupe of Galician dancers – nine of them, all ladies, were whirling in a frenzy like their Turkish counterparts. Their wails pitched higher and higher piercing my head so that I had to clamp my hands over my ears to shut out the awful howls. A young man nearby jeered at me. Despite my unsteady legs I took a swing at him, missed and fell, hitting my chin on the ground and biting my tongue. I got up and scurried away like a dog. The blood in my mouth tasted strange. Thick and oily.

When I reached Xosé I was in something of a state. I could see from my friends' faces they were disturbed. I however felt no concern for them. I was now experiencing an unquenchable thirst. I ordered a large wine, red, and drank it down immediately, ordering more.

On the table were a number of small olive and potato tapas. I ignored them and went for the bloody ham, consuming the entire dish without offering it around. Then another wine.

Xosé had never seen me like this before and I think it was with some relief that he greeted Hank who arrived about thirty minutes later. I introduced them and set off for the toilets as now I was wracked by vicious cramps in my stomach.

When I returned to the table it was clear something had passed between Hank and Xosé for they turned to stare at me. Tatiana had disappeared.

Xosé suggested we move on and I quickly agreed.

I remember finishing my wine, trying to get to my feet, but found myself overcome with an extreme fatigue. I then recall leaning on Xosé and Hank as we made our way through a warren of tiny streets that seemed to go on forever, until we reached a final bar. This was smaller and darker and had little atmosphere. But it did have a couch and it was upon this that they laid me down as the pains in my stomach grew stronger and I cried out for ... I don't know what for. I only know that I was seized by some wild passion, a desire and urge that had me struggling against my bonds. For they had tied me down. A man in black entered the room and looked at me. He gently lifted my head and held a drink to my lips, for which I was grateful and consumed very quickly. Whilst I drank he spoke some words, I think in Italian, though at the time I thought it Latin. I was aware of other people singing, chanting, and the smell of incense in the bar. Then the darkness that lurked in the corners came out and drew me into it.

I have only a faint memory of the horrors I saw there – a million faces contorted with terror, a beast – something dark and winged and hairy – called to me. I struggled with my sense of self and felt part of it dissolve. There were lights and candles and a precipice, which tugged me closer and closer to the edge, until the priest's words cut through my dream.

When I came round I found myself in a shuttered room with only a bed and a chest of drawers upon which stood a glass of water.

I drank it and sat up. When I opened the door, light flooded in. As my eyes became accustomed to it I saw that I was outside a dusty church, nowhere near the city. On the pavement in front was a familiar camper van.

'Welcome back to the world,' Hank greeted me.

He wouldn't tell me much as we drove back to A Coruña but I gathered that I had experienced some kind of mental breakdown, a result of my difficult divorce no doubt, and was reassured that it was quite to be expected and nothing to be ashamed of. It had, however, resulted in startling hallucinations and delirium that required sedation. For some reason, which he wouldn't reveal, this had taken place in a monastery. Hank muttered something about the vagaries of medical insurance but I didn't believe him.

When we reached the hotel, he waited outside while I packed, then in silence he drove me to the airport in Santiago de Compostela to get the next flight home.

As I got out of the car, he told me, 'You might have been saved but you're marked. You can't come back here, right?'

And I replied to him, 'I know.'

I never saw Madness in A Coruña.

At least, I never saw the band.

CHRISTMAS EVE AT THE WITCH MUSEUM

It was Christmas Eve at the Witch Museum and all
*   through the house*
Everyone was stirring, even the mouse,
For the season of goodwill ain't limited to sapiens and
*   their cats*
But extends to all creatures including rodents and
*   rodent-looking bats,*
The Hedgewitch in her corner was decked with mistletoe,
And if I chanced on ~~Sam~~ someone near it I planned
*   to snog them, ho ho ho.*

Mmm. I put the pen down and set off. Could I get away with that? I mean, bats to my mind at least did look a lot like mice. Winged mice. And mice were categorised in the rodent bracket. Still, I wasn't sure that line was scanning properly.

Did it matter anyway? I wondered. I mean, it was only a *gesture*.

The idea was to thank everybody for coming and to read out something so hilarious it would tickle their funny muscles and kick off the party good and proper. However, as I came into the newly cleared Talks Area, I thought it was already cooking nicely.

It had taken them a week, but eventually Bronson and Sam had managed to stack up all the chairs and tables and lodge them in a cellar. There were a lot of them, I had discovered. Cellars that is. Full of exhibits and models in varying states of preservation. I'd stopped counting rooms after number seventeen but my new year's resolution was to find out exactly how many there were and what they contained. The task didn't fill me with joy, I had to admit.

Once Bronson and Sam had stowed the paraphernalia from the Talks Area away, a large party space emerged, which they then proceeded to decorate in a manner which may well have turned gaudy, possibly even vulgar, had I not inserted myself into the role of executive producer JUST IN TIME. Gone now were the mains-powered plastic snowmen, the self-inflating eight-foot reindeer, a nodding Jesus and the giant rusting Santa's sleigh. The latter they had adorned with models of evil-looking sprites and imps which Bronson had retrieved from an ex-display case in the basement. Sam had also wedged a red pillowcase full of Tupperware boxes into the driving seat and inserted a rather mournful Green Man behind it. He'd put a whip in his hand and fastened upon his head a fur-trimmed hat that had a white beard suspended on elastic. This fluttered about in the various (and many) draughts, lending the nature spirit an air of animation. But even so, the green mannequin was not fooling anyone into thinking he was Santa. Last week I'd extricated him from the sleigh and hauled him into the lobby so he now formed part of a kind of unholy Magi. Positioned beside a dusty Saint Nicholas and a horned Krampus with chains and bells, the three figures gazed down upon a straw-filled manger that contained a little blonde baby doll. Unfortunately, they really did look like they were going to eat it. There had been a couple of complaints, but we were a Witch Museum for God's sake. If kids were scared of a few old legends like those, then there was no way they were going to make it past the Medieval anus-crackers.

Didn't pacify the parents, unfortunately, but you can't please all the people all the time, right?

Under my instructions the Santa sleigh had been dragged out and placed at the side of the museum entrance, thus creating a show of festive frippery that you could see from the road. In fact, it was the only source of illumination once the few street lights in Hobleythick Lane were turned off at ten o'clock. The consequences of which meant it constituted a nice bit of advertising to passing motorists and random pedestrians on their way home from the pub. Bronson ran an outdoor electricity cable to it, so I was able to decorate the sledge with lots of LED parcel-shaped ornaments, outdoor fairy lights and a couple of flashing reindeers. Personally, I thought the cable that ran from the ticket office to the sleigh, should be taped down for Health and Safety reasons, but the caretaker insisted it was fine. The whole thing lit it up gloriously, only sparking on occasion when it got damp. When that happened, however, it conjured a scene from *Final*

Destination, which was literally electrifying. Still, Bronson was convinced it was okay, so I let it go.

Instead of all the tawdry rubbish in the Talks Area, I cut holly and ivy from the garden and decked the hall with boughs and boughs of the stuff, as per the jolly carol. Lengths of icicles criss-crossed the ceiling, transforming the place into a glittering arctic forest, in the middle of which I had suspended a giant wreath fashioned from twigs, holly, gold-sprayed leaves, a dilapidated giant wooden star and mistletoe. Quite the centrepiece, I thought. I'd come across a bunch of grimy wicker stars in another cellar so gave them a bit of a dust and hung them around the garland on varying lengths of ribbon, so you could not miss the mistletoe should you be intending to spread your goodwill and clamp your smackers on that special someone. Not that I had such things on my mind when I erected it, you understand. Oh no no no.

There were more decorations round the sides of the room. After Krampus-gate I decided to cover up the panels that illustrated particularly nasty episodes of our county's history: burning heretics tended to put people off their flame-grilled chicken wings. In order to maintain appetites, I had sello-taped sheets of Christmas wrapping paper over the panels. It was only this evening, as I'd given the room a final sweep, that I noticed someone had cut peepholes so that the witches and martyrs could join in and watch our celebratory shenanigans. Which was very considerate if you thought about it. And also a bit weird. Then again, weird stuff was the norm here, which I was just about getting used to.

The focal point of the Talks Area, however, was most

certainly the stage. Specifically, the magnificent Christmas tree. Oh, how it sparkled and shined. At least seven feet high, it had been brought in by a donor, who shall remain anonymous on account of the fact they had half-inched it from the grounds of Howlet Hall, the manor of the local Lord. Seeing as that old git was now behind bars for his foiled attempt to murder my good self, and various other shocking depravities that involved my mother and grandma, I thought a tree from his grounds was the least he could bloody do. In terms of reparation it was actually pretty light-weight, legal or not. No one outside of the Witch Museum team knew where it had come from, so Edward de Vere was never going to find out. And it was a beauty. I had decked it with baubles, lashings of twinkling lights, fake snow and various trinkets we found in a box of Christmas decorations. They included a pretty woven snow-flake, a knitted kitty that almost resembled Hecate, our museum cat, wearing a stripy scarf (not that she would ever do something so undignified), and a large, gnome-like figure that might have been a voodoo poppet in a previous incarnation. A couple of Wiccans had kindly sent us some hand-decorated glass balls, which I'd stuck straight on. We'd had something else come through the letterbox a day later. The gift completely baffled me when I unwrapped it, but then I worked out it must be a local custom to donate tree decorations to the museum. It looked like a tooth embedded in a chunk of meat, with dubious brown stains around the base but, seriously, it's amazing what a job lot of glitter can do. You didn't notice it hanging there on the lower branches anyway. Not really.

Trace and Vanessa had done us proud with a buffet table that sagged under the banquet of seasonal goodies, and which, currently, a large contingent of the scout and girl guide leaders were tucking into. I had brought in some outside bar staff so the museum's team could have a bit of a well-earned knees-up. It looked, however, like this agency had supplied work experience applicants. The adolescent catering assistants were blanching beneath their pimples, blinking rapidly and staring at everyone in a manner that suggested they were … what's the word? Ah yes – scared. Still, as long as they were topping up the glasses properly. That was the main thing.

I didn't really know what their problem was. I mean, everyone was just letting their hair down. Well, a lot of Adder's Forkers were. Carmen Constable and her vegetarian boyfriend, Florian, were jigging with the middle-aged village bombshell, Neighbour Val. Emboldened by fizz, Terry Bridgewater was doing his best to impress Molly Acton from the neighbouring farm. Audrey, the resident protester, and the woman I had named 'Pink Anorak' but who was called Anne by everyone else, had their eyes fixed on the dancefloor. They were doing a half-arsed job of looking disapproving, unaware their feet were twitching to the rhythm of the tune. I followed their gaze over to a laudable demonstration of what can go wrong when you allow geriatric drinkers priority access to the bar. The elderly man, known to the entire community of Adder's Fork as 'Granddad', was enacting something that resembled a cross between an aggressive Morris routine and 'The Birdy Dance'. His elbow-flapping, butt-twerking partner was Molly's dad, Bob. Bob Acton's pitchfork clanged with surprising volume against Granddad's aluminium crutch, as the two formed a lopsided arch under which the various Adder's Fork revellers were ducking and whooping.

Representatives from the local constabulary, the newly promoted Inspector Sue Scrub, PCs Dennis Bean and Shaun O'Neil, stood apart, watching and clapping. They all had fixed grins buttoned onto their faces but Scrub was coming across like a resigned gazelle at a rabid tiger convention. At least they were here, fostering community relationships, though I was sure Bean and O'Neil would prefer to be anywhere else but.

Sergeant Bobby Brown had made an appearance too. The bloke, regularly as cool as a cucumber, was staring at the dancers unblinkingly whilst scribbling in his notebook (without looking down – impressive). Chloe Brown, the gothy forensic lecturer who volunteered here, was inching over to him with a drink in each hand. They weren't related, as far as I knew, but it looked like Chloe was hoping to get familiar. Go Chloe, I thought and wondered if she stood a chance.

Someone grabbed my hand and tugged me towards the pitchfork/crutch arch.

I was surprised to see it was Sam.

'Come here,' he said and pulled me into the centre of the room.

Was it the mistletoe he was heading for?

'Oh really?' I responded with a little eyelash flutter.

Sam jerked his head to the stage where my auntie was

decked in enough sequins and flashing earrings to make the Christmas tree feel underdressed. 'Do you think Babs could play something less *paganey*?' he asked.

'For God's sake, Sam,' I said and rolled my eyes. 'It's *The Pogues*!'

'Yes, but look at them,' he said, as Granddad hopped past me with a pair of barbecue tongs held high. I didn't know where he had got them from. I hadn't put any out on the table. Oh God. I hoped that they were barbecue tongs and made a mental note to check the Heretics Fork display later.

'Yeah, well,' I said. 'That's just them, isn't it?' and shrugged. 'The Adder's Forkers. They're ebullient.'

'Hmmm,' said Sam and frowned. I didn't know why. Then he stopped walking and let go of my arm. 'Could be this, you know,' and he pointed up at the wreath.

Mistletoe.

Bingo.

Was love, at last, coming through the air tonight?

'Well!' I said and leaned in steeply. 'Seems rude not to.' And then I puckered my lips.

But Sam didn't look at all romantic. At least he didn't look like he had any romantic intentions. Unless having romantic intentions made him squint his eyes, crunch his brow and make a circular motion with his finger. In which case, I could see why he was still single.

Either way, I wasn't letting the opportunity slip through my fingers. That had happened far too often. I sashayed my hips and jiggled my bum sexily. It *is* possible to jiggle sexily, you see. I'm living proof.

'This is no time to start prancing round like a pillock,' Sam said tetchily.

I tutted. 'I'm not prancing, I'm dancing ...'

'Oh,' he said, then looked at me hard. 'Not you as well?'

'What d'you mean "as well"?'

'Are you feeling . . . er . . . excitable, Rosie?'

I took a deep breath. 'Always around you, Sam.'

But he just laughed and said, 'I don't know how to take that.'

I was going to tell him he could take it whichever way he wanted but before I could get it out he said, 'I think it might be having an effect. There's an energy in here.'

'What?' I asked, wondering if he had sprayed on a particularly attractive aftershave. 'What's having an effect?'

'The ceremonial circle you've drawn. It's likely to have triggered a response. Even if only a psychological one.'

That stopped me.

I stared at him. 'How do you mean – drawn?'

'Big circle,' he said pointing to the outer ring of icicles. 'With this pentacle at its centre, encompassing the wreath, which of course presents a double circle. Very powerful symbology.'

'What pentacle?' I said looking up and into the garland above us. 'That's just some old star I cable-tied onto the ivy.'

'No, it's not,' said Sam. 'It's the Pendragon Pentagram. I wondered where it had gone. Not sure what century it dates back to, but it's carved with Enochian symbols thought to aid communication with angels.' He frowned again. 'Or other supernatural entities with far less integrity. Generally, it can be used to summon a spirit or traverse celestial planes etc.'

'Oh-er,' I said.

'Yes, Rosie.' Sam cleared his throat and took a deep breath, which always signified a bit of a lecture was on its way. 'And these rural pentagrams you've added around it do amplify old Pendragon's purpose. They might look like simple compositions, but they would have been woven with a perfect focus on magic. The outcome that the craftsman—'

'Or craftswoman.'

'Yes, the outcome that he or she wished to achieve – protection, fertility – it's in there. Most of the villagers will be aware of it. One can almost feel energy radiating out of the pentacles.'

'Antique wicker stars,' I muttered, looking at them. How was I supposed to know? They looked like shabby-chic decorations to me. 'Yeah, well. It's Christmas. Everyone's excited. And anyway, all that pentacle/symbol malarkey, well, we both know that's likely to be a load of hocus pocus isn't it? I mean this stuff doesn't really work.'

'Well, there's frequently a psychological effect,' said Sam and grinned. 'And to be honest, we've never tried out the Pendragon Pentagram, have we?'

'There's a lot of things we haven't tried,' I said and winked. 'But if we were going to start with one, then this wouldn't be my first choi—'

In front of me, Sam clapped his hands over his ears.

A terrible screech filled the Talks Area as a stylus skidded across vinyl. Everyone winced collectively and stopped what they were doing.

All heads turned towards the decks on the stage where Tone Bridgewater was wrestling the mic out of Auntie Babs' hand.

Swatting Auntie Babs away, Tone managed to free the microphone and wheezed into it. 'Quick everyone! You'll never believe it, but there's a demon outside!'

By the time we had all stampeded out of the Talks Area, through the folklore section, round the hedgewitch, across the Blackly Be exhibit, stopped and checked our reflections in the 'There but for the Grace of God' hall of mirrors, grimaced past the torture display and burst through the 'Abandon all Hope' door over the lobby and into the front garden – there was no one there.

No one, that is, apart from Bronson.

The caretaker was lying in the middle of the path, flat on his back. His bucket, kicked to one side, rolled gently back and forth.

'Oh my God!' said Sam and I together and darted to his side. Neighbour Val appeared out of the crowd and flung herself over Bronson, neatly elbowing me out of the way. She had a habit of doing that. I shuffled round his shoulders and put my head to his chest, listening for a heartbeat.

'Crikey!' said Sam.

'I'm not dead yet,' said Bronson. Loudly.

'Oh thank the lord for that,' cried Neighbour Val and for

some reason began fanning herself. 'What you doing down here, Brons?'

Sam gave me a look and I knew instantly he was as surprised as me by Val's shortening of our colleague's name. It betrayed intimacy. Yet the salty old dog hadn't mentioned any dalliances to us. Then again, he was a man of few words.

Tone Bridgewater had caught up with the herd and popped out of it to inform us. 'He must have been floored by the demon.'

'I tell you what,' said Bronson as Sam and Val pulled him into a sitting position. 'It came at me with some force. Well, *over* me.'

'What did?' I said, finding it hard to take the whole demon thing on board.

'I dunno,' said Bronson. 'One minute it was here, the next it was gone.' He shrugged. 'Just like that.'

'But what was *it* exactly?' asked Sam again, then clarified. 'What did it look like?'

Tone had come over and squatted down beside us. 'I saw it out the side of my eye,' he said. 'When I was having a, er, fag. Didn't realise Bronson was out here too.'

'And?' I said.

Tone nodded and pulled his coat tighter round him. 'It's dark and it was too.'

'It was dark too?' Sam tried to pin him down, metaphorically speaking. 'You mean someone wearing dark-coloured clothes?'

'Sort of. They were flapping.' Tone swallowed. 'But it weren't no man.'

'Oh for gawd's sake how do you know it weren't no man if he had clothes on? It weren't a cow or a pig in drag, was it?' Neighbour Val giggled inappropriately.

'No, it weren't,' said Tone in a grave voice and shook his head. 'Because as far as I'm aware, pigs don't *fly*.'

'This is Adder's Fork,' I muttered. 'You just might not have clocked them.'

'It flew?' Sam dragged his eyes away from Bronson and regarded Tone with fascination.

But it was Bronson who nodded. 'Felt that way to me too, son. Could hear a swooshing. Breeze.'

There was a murmuring over by the museum entrance then a voice raised into a wail.

'The wages of sin.' Oh God it was Audrey. Her creaky voice grew higher, '"For the wages of sin is death; but the gift of God is eternal life through Jesus Christ our Lord" amen. Repent whilst you still have time. Repent on the eve that Jesus Christ is born.'

She never missed a trick, that one.

'He flew down, out of nowhere, then sprang off again,' Tone explained ignoring Audrey's warning. 'Up, up into the sky.'

'Seriously though,' called Nicky from the Village Shop, who was standing beside Audrey. 'If it's attacked Bronson someone should call the police.'

'We're here,' said Scrub shoving her way to the front of the crowd.

'Bloody hell! That was quick,' Neighbour Val marvelled.

Bobby Brown decided to take control with a 'Nothing

to see here, please disperse.' It had absolutely no effect on anyone. But Chloe had followed him out and added, 'There's still 45 minutes left of that free bar,' which seemed to do the trick. That and the fact that PCs Bean and O' Neil started shepherding them.

'I knew it,' said Inspector Scrub as she flicked her notebook open. 'This place, you two,' she eyeballed me and Sam, 'and those Forkers. There weren't any way tonight was going to go without a hitch.' And she asked Bronson to start at the beginning.

Once his statement had been taken down by Scrub, Bronson was led off by Neighbour Val, who I noted stuck her shoulder under his armpit and tucked his arm around her waist. Sam suggested they find the brandy in the office and both of them complied with relative enthusiasm, ignoring the titter from Audrey who was still hovering by the door.

'What about you, Tone?' Scrub asked. 'Can you elaborate any further?'

'I'm trying to think,' he said and tapped his forehead on the side.

'Don't hurt yourself,' Scrub said.

'He was taller than me, by some height. I think he might have had a hat on, which kinda made him seem bigger. Maybe like a toff hat. No, what's it called – a top hat,' he said. The boy was trying hard. Maybe he was compensating for that stuff back in the summer with the break-ins and the flowers and the ghost and that. Long story. Whatever, something was working inside that closely cropped skullcap.

'He was dark. The clothes were dark,' Tone squinted. 'There was swishing, like curtains opening suddenly.'

'Good,' said Sam. 'You're doing really well. Could it have been a cloak?'

Tone closed his eyes then nodded. 'Could have been. The moon was just clouding over so I didn't get a good look.'

I looked up at the sky. It was completely covered now. In fact, I could feel a drizzle starting in the air.

'But there was light coming out of him.' Tone went on shaking his head, dismissing the words with incredulity even as they tumbled from his mouth.

'Light?' I said and felt my eyebrows tug together. Quickly I put my fingers to my brow and smoothed them. You could end up with a permanently unflattering crease there, if you weren't careful.

'Yeah,' Tone said, nodding slowly and pulled the recollection closer.

I pressed on, with a consciously unwrinkled forehead. 'How? How was there light coming out of him.'

'It was blue. Like flames,' said Tone carefully.

'Interesting,' said Sam.

Scrub raised her eyebrows. 'Really? Sounds suspicious to me.'

Sam nodded. 'It's remarkably similar to an urban legend from the nineteenth century: Spring-heeled Jack. Have you heard of him?'

We all shook our heads and waited for him to share his brains.

'Started in the East End but actually did come down here

to Essex,' he began, tapping his chin as he spoke. 'All over the country, in fact. He was said to be, by turns, a devil, a ghost, a demon, as Tone correctly asserted, and a bull!'

'Sounds like bull,' I muttered quietly.

'What?' said Tone. 'Like a cow? It weren't no cow, I can tell you that.'

'No,' said Sam and continued on. 'Witnesses described him as being able to leap great distances.'

'That's true,' said Tone.

'He was alleged to breathe out blue flames and had claws for hands that he would attack people with. Some thought it was a hoax but there were multiple sightings from 1828 to 1904.'

It had grown quiet outside as Sam spoke and we all jumped as an owl hooted in one of the bordering pines.

'He was shot at several times, but with no effect,' Sam went on, his own voice dropping to a whisper as if he didn't want to be overheard. 'Some commentators believe Spring-heeled Jack was the rakish Lord Henry de la Poer Beresford, the third Marquis of Waterford. Certainly, the aristocrat had the means and mischievous nature to have the costumes made. He was spry too. Athletic. Of course, others believe Spring-heeled Jack was a paranormal creature, possibly an extra-terrestrial entity with a non-human appearance, who had slipped through a portal from a high-gravity dimension and was, therefore, less affected by the standard rules of physics on Earth.'

'Ha ha ha ha ha.'

A low cackle echoed round the garden.

I tensed and surveyed the pines, the front wall, the fields to the Acton's farm. There was no one there that I could see, though it was pretty hard to get clarity beyond the circle of illumination radiating from the sleigh.

'Who's that?' said Scrub, looking up and down each side of the garden. She raised her voice higher. 'Come out and show yourself.'

As if daring her, the laughter grew in volume, projecting through the trees across the expanse of garden. At once, from somewhere over our heads, there came a terrific whoosh and a large black thing dropped from the sky and hit the gravel beyond us.

Little pebbles flew up into the air, which seemed, just then, to crackle with electricity.

Then, to my utter astonishment the darkness was lit up by a burst of blue flame.

In that moment I saw the silhouette of a very, very tall figure who, as Tone had accurately described, was dressed in ghastly black robes – a tatty cape perhaps. I had little time to take much in because all at once it sprang up again, in a steep and graceful arc, that reached its apex above the front wall and then dropped down into the lane just as the street lights switched off.

Before you could say 'council cutbacks', Bobby Brown, whose reflexes were clearly also not of this world, raced down the path and out of the Witch Museum in hot pursuit.

'Oh my God,' said Chloe, who I had just realised was standing next to me, lightly holding the sleeve of my dress. 'What the hell was that?'

Sam's voice had become raspy. 'If I'm not mistaken, that was Spring-heeled Jack.'

'I told you,' said Tone, his voice betraying a quiver.

Despite myself a shudder rippled down my spine.

'That can't be a demon,' said Scrub and began to stalk towards the wall where the creature disappeared. 'I won't have it.'

I couldn't see her face from this angle but I thought it likely that her eyes were narrowed to thin slits and her mouth screwed into a knot of absolute determination. It was an expression I had encountered in the past, as if her sheer force of will was going to unmask the ghostly form we'd all just witnessed and prove it completely un-demon-like.

'Er, should we?' Sam gestured towards the lane.

'No,' said Chloe. 'He's already coming back.'

And he was indeed. Bobby Brown and Scrub were jogging back to us.

'IC1, I reckon,' said Bobby Brown. 'Caught a glimpse of white under a hood, in the facial area. Exceptional height, maybe eight feet.'

'You sure?' said Scrub.

Bobby nodded. 'Do you want me to call it in?'

'Mm,' said Scrub and turned back to us. 'We've got Bean and O'Neil here. Phone them.'

Bobby took his mobile out of his pocket and began to stab it when we all heard another whooshing sound.

Again everyone froze.

Scrub muttered, 'You're having a laugh.'

And, bang, the leaping black thing plopped down right next to Brown.

One had to admire the audacity.

Again there was a flash. A purpley, bluey flame, thinner this time. Then, I heard a light metallic tinkling and the spectre leapt up impressively, soaring over our heads, and landed, with a skitter, on the roof of the lobby.

'Good God,' exclaimed Sam.

'Wages of sin!' wailed Audrey, who was cantering out of the shadows to stare at our unearthly visitor along with the rest of us. 'Your doing,' she waved her finger at me. 'All that meddling with dark magic and witches, you have brought the demons in.'

Tone, who I had forgotten was here, spoke up. 'Actually,' he said. 'It don't really look like a demon now.'

And he was right. The thing on the roof was pretty humanoid in form, having two arms, a large torso and a head. Though said head did seem extraordinarily large and was crowned with, as Tone had correctly identified, a black top hat. Obscuring much of its bulk was a flippy flappy floaty cloaky thing, from the bottom of which protruded two limbs that were unmistakably legs. Though they were, indeed, very long ones.

'He's got my phone!' said Bobby. Muttering something I didn't understand but which plausibly was a slew of international swear words, he made to sprint after the thing. Scrub however stayed him.

'Hang about, Bobs,' she said. 'What goes up must come down. And look – left leg. Below the knee.'

Up on the roof, the creature could be seen in silhouette. The lower part of a ragged trouser leg had detached itself, gaping to reveal a glint of metal reflecting the flashing lights of the sleigh just beneath it. 'Could that be a section of nifty aluminium stilt I see before me?'

'It could indeed, ma'm,' said Brown, straightening himself up.

The 'demon' gave a little bounce and giggled.

'Jumping stilts! That would explain the giant leaps,' agreed Sam.

I bent my ears to it and caught the scratchy coil and recoil of shunting springs. The sound was definitely not issuing from the creature's heels but higher up around the calf and knee joint. Which, to my mind, confirmed it was a solid, man-made mechanism that was helping Master S.H. Jack achieve his astonishing height. I was no longer close-minded or discomfited when it came to the presentation of unusual phenomena, it was true, but the notion of demons from another dimension had played havoc with my comfort zone.

'You,' shouted Scrub at him, in her finest cease-and-desist-with-the-fuckwittery voice. 'Return the phone at once.'

Again, a titter carried across the night air. The rooftop fiend spread its cloak, which I now saw had been designed to resemble two giant bat wings, and burped. Then rather unexpectedly, it broke into song:

'With a skip and a leap of his spit-heeled boots,' he trilled,

'By night and stars across old London town's roofs,

The folk do quake, the folk do quiver but the folk must watch their backs,

Because the beast's behind you – he's Spring-heeled Jack.'

A dramatic punctuation to the end of the verse was formed by a burst of blue flame, which issued from so-called 'Jack's' mouth.

It was, if nothing else, spectacular, and prompted Chloe to give out a little cry. Sam gasped and began to clap. Audrey smirked at him and made a loud proclamation about the devil and his false prophet in lakes of burning sulphur.

But Scrub was unimpressed. 'Very good. Now hand it over. It belongs to my officer friend here.'

But the joker on the roof went on unheeding, 'Like a devil,' it sang picking up on Audrey's charming motif, and giving one of its legs a high kick. 'Like a fiend, like a black angel ...'

'My POLICE officer, friend here,' Scrub bellowed.

'The ghostly spectre of . . . oh . . .' the singer petered out, his voice now rather weakened by the revelation of agents of the law in the audience. 'Police? Officer, you say?' He was definitely human.

'That's right,' said Scrub.

This had a further sobering effect on Mr Jack who said, 'Oh,' and tottered lightly down the sloping roof to the right-hand side of the lobby. 'I didn't realise there was such esteemed company in your gathering.'

Some of his words were slurred. As he reached the edge of the lobby roof and was therefore closer to the light that radiated from our decorations, I noticed his footing was a little less than firm.

'I'll bet,' said Bobby and began to approach the porch.

'Come down now sir, please. Right away.' Like Scrub, he had a voice that conjured images of lonely cells, gruel and hot blisters.

'Well, when you put it like that,' the bloke on the roof conceded. 'My chariot awaits!' He gave a non-flammable sigh then bent his knees and leapt.

There was a loud 'boing' as he rocketed into the air perhaps two metres then, as I realised where he was intending to land, my mouth opened in alarm. 'Noooo,' I began to howl. 'It's not safe.'

Out of the corner of my eye I could see Sam had worked it out too and was raising his arms in warning. Whoever it was in the Spring-heeled Jack get-up had not properly thought this move through. I guess he anticipated that landing in the front seat of the sleigh might be a fantastic finale to his performance tonight. Of course he didn't know about Bronson's dodgy cable or the sparking that started up when it got damp, like it was now.

I remember hearing a 'Geronimo!' Then there was an 'ooff', a bang and a terrific sizzle. The sleigh flashed one last time and then exploded into sparks.

Smoke filled the air.

For a moment no one moved, then Audrey careered across the path to the smoking wreck. 'Geoffrey! Geoffrey!' she screamed. 'Somebody do something.'

Scrub and Bobby Brown, quicker than the rest of us, dived into the tangle of metal and began tugging it apart, finally wrenching a lightly smoking form from the wreckage.

'Sorry about that,' it said.

At least it was alive.

'Oh heavens,' said Audrey, buzzing around it with a hair scarf in her hand, batting at his form as if putting out invisible flames. 'Geoffrey are you all right?'

'I think so,' said the sooty figure now established as Geoffrey, whom Scrub and Bobby were leading to the lobby steps.

'Should I fetch Doctor Patel?' Chloe Brown asked.

Audrey whirled round and poked a finger at me. 'Happy now?'

'I'll get Doctor Patel,' said Chloe and made off into the museum.

'Should turn this off. Plug in the lobby?' Tone asked but then followed Chloe in without waiting for an answer.

'Look what you've done to him, the poor boy,' Audrey continued, helping Scrub and Bobby settle 'Geoffrey' down on the steps.

'Done to him!' I said, outrage filling my boots. 'No one made him jump around like that. On private property.'

'Well, he looks like he's relatively unscathed,' said Scrub. 'Nothing damaged.'

'Apart from my pride,' said a smudged Geoffrey.

'And my bloody sleigh!' I said, surveying the wreckage. There was only one blackened reindeer standing.

'It's a hazard,' said Audrey and came at me again. 'You shouldn't have it out here anyway. I've seen it sparking.'

Regrettably, I looked at my feet. Should have done a risk assessment. Though possibly leaping stilt-jumpers wouldn't have come up on it anyway.

'What on earth were you doing, er, Geoffrey?' Sam asked the guy and stepped in front of me, blocking Audrey's advance.

Geoffrey lifted his face to us. 'I was only trying out my routine. I'm hoping to show it at the London Dungeon. Auntie Audrey said you'd be a willing crowd and I thought – it's a Witch Museum – why not? I'm available for hire, you know.'

'The cheek of it!' Sam tutted.

'How much?' I asked quickly, keen not to enter into a discussion over public liability.

'Er, £100 a go.'

Good, I thought: a starting bid. 'Right, well, you can do a couple of spins when we reopen in January. Consider it some well-needed practice. And that'll be free, thank you very much. Compensation for the damage.'

Geoffrey puffed out an indignant, 'Don't think so.'

I nodded at Scrub. 'Then book him, Danno.'

Scrub sniffed. 'You should be spending a night in the cells. A criminal damage charge might dent your sense of humour.'

Sam grinned and added, 'Knocking over Bronson. Not to mention trespass.'

'Public land,' Geoffrey tendered but his voice was lacking in conviction.

'No, it's not,' I told him. 'It's mine. And you, Audrey, you should be ashamed of yourself. Getting your nephew in on this. Do you want him to have a criminal record?'

Audrey's face was still pinched but she said nothing and at that moment Chloe returned with Dr Patel.

'Right then,' said Scrub. 'We'll get the doctor to check you then I'll take you two home. Perhaps we should go over the terms of your injunction, Audrey?'

She opened her mouth but then shut it and I think I saw her nod.

Bobby Brown asked the inspector if she needed him, but Scrub said she'd be just fine and would probably get off home to the wife after this. The sergeant nodded and then, for the first time ever, I saw him smile. At Chloe. Who smiled right back.

Perhaps love *was* in the air tonight.

'Right,' said Scrub. 'You lot go back inside. You've got guests to entertain.'

'Well, they'll certainly be thrilled by this little tale,' said Sam.

'Mm. Rather unusual and not very Christmassy,' I said as we headed into the lobby.

'Oh, I dunno,' Sam jerked his head back to the sleigh. 'Lords a-leaping are quite festive, aren't they?'

'A tad more than demons and celestial gateways.'

And then he laughed. 'Now where were we before Spring-heeled Jack stole the show?'

'Underneath the mistletoe,' I said with a wink.

'That's right,' he said and took my hand. 'So we were.'

BAREFOOT THROUGH
THE SNOW

I can only but think that the governor, no, not the governor
– the lord. Yes. I can only but think that the lord – not he
in heaven – but he in the seat who judged me so – that the
lord has felt his frozen heart thaw. Even in this midwinter
bitterness.

What a time for it to be so.

But nothing surprises me any longer. The worst is come
and gone.

So cold. So bone chilling.

And yet my resolve will not falter. My feet, hard upon
the crisping snow, will march on and on. Under this night
guided by the bare-knuckle moon, over pale fields, I come to
you, my dearlings. Can you hear me? Edmund, my strong
boy. And Christabel, oh so sweet. I will gaze upon your lovely
face once more, my child.

And though I have no gifts to bring, I shall hold you in my
arms and I shall breathe in your milky softness.

The soft glow of you in swaddling always did bring in the
light. Even in that most black of hells, that place crammed

with lice and prickly darkness. And wailing and poison and death and beating . . . no. I will not linger on it.

For, look – I am out.

The chill is not so bad on my feet. I cannot feel them beneath me. Though I did not guess I would live to walk across snow again, see the naked trees, the silver leaves, the sparkling stars.

Oh what a heaven is this.

Free.

He must have seen that Roger was not straight, that the Francks had their fingers right in him. William's wife has never suffered us since Margaret did roll with him two years since. She is a lewd woman indeed, my sister Margaret, but so fair of face that none can resist her charms. In a way it is bewitchment, I suppose. Perhaps they were right – she did enchant those gentlemen. And yet it is I they accuse with more hate. I, who was dealt with by the lord so harshly – condemned to death after I birthed my child. They would not hang me with unborn life in my belly. Though once birthed, they did say I would be soon upon the gallows. Me! When Margaret is saucier by far. She was inside but for a half year in the end. Six times in the stocks to follow.

But then, I must wager, her reprieve did help. She took in my Edmund from Goodwife Foster and looked after him as if he were her own. Then when I had birthed lovely Christabel in the dungeon low, it was my sister who came to me, who fetched my dearling to nurse and love, so she would not rot down there with me. With the rats and the lice and the . . . no . . . no. Not to think on it. Not to think on it now that I am out here, with the stars in my hair and the spire of Haven in near sight.

Mother would have taken them, cared for Christabel and Edmund. But they led her out from the Assize and put a rope around her neck, then strung her up to the gallows tree. They swung her back and forth till she was dead. Just an old lady. Ladies, to be fair: Mother and Johanna Upney and Joan Prentice. The Three Joans, they did call them. All the land did hear of their false witchery. Bitter, bitter now. Though my relations to them did bestow a certain notoriety. The gaoler did beat me less, and not for pity.

A beast, perhaps a wolf cries in the distance and I am pulled back into the fields. In the moonlight they gleam, though I cannot see the beast on them. He may be near, or he may be far. The blanket of snow does muffle the howl, so I cannot tell. But, peculiar now, I have no fear. Not of the beast. No. Though there is a beginning in my soul. Something uncertain and movable fast, like a moth caught in a jar, who knows it should be free.

No, do not think on it.

Put one foot in front of the other. Then follow on with the next.

For how long, I wonder, have I walked like this – barefoot over snow? I cannot recall it. Nor how I came to be in my finest robe, clean and bright, and not clad in the soiled prison shift. There are holes in my remembering, deep like warrens, where nothing grows but a vast emptiness, dark, as if a candle had just been snuffed out. For a moment the hollows threaten to take me. And at once dread creeps forward, like a hunter, ready to snare, and I feel my heart quicken. But I harden myself against it and shake my head and skip and look up and that is when I sight it. On the hill, Three Tree Wood. I can see the outline of the distant yews that give the rise its name. And I remember it a landmark. Yes, a marker to Margaret's village. And instead of letting the brute, Fear, into my breast I realise I am . . . happy.

For Haven is near.

My feet quicken at the notion and very soon I am past the hill. In the near distance the cottages cluster. I pass the Glasscocks' house, with its tall chimneys and its paddock. They were rich. They did not have to accuse Joan Prentice so. I am sorry for their loss, but Joan did only mutter a curse, and I do not believe a muttering can kill a child. But I muttered too. Curses a plenty. And they say that I did lame Jeremiah Browne.

I did not wish him well, it is true. That spiteful old man had a sharp tongue and was wont to use it whenever he could. He never approved of Margaret and I unwed so. With our children. But the men that should be husbands would not be. So how may that be our fault? Or that of the children? They should not be blamed for the sin of their fathers. But Jeremiah Browne did not care. And he did turn out our bastards when they came knocking on his door for bread. And he did raise his stick and take it to them with vigour. Margaret's Thomas and my poor Edmund could not walk for a week. And so I said, I wished that Jeremiah would be visited by the same pain and languish such as that he inflicted on our sons.

I did not know it would come true.

'Tis God that did it. For I have never seen the Devil in my cottage. Never.

The houses in Haven are grander than my humble home. Though there are some like the cottage I brought up my Edmund in, you can see that this village has more coin in it. The walls are whitewashed so fine. Some have lanterns fastened there. Some are even alight! How can they frame wasting that oil? There are folk who have more coin than reason. Or perhaps it is the dwelling of a watchman not yet returned home, seeking the light to guide him safe.

But it is so hushed. Everyone be inside, at this hour, tucked into their beds, warm and sleepful.

Even the tavern is quiet. And that do make a surprise.

The lights are out inside. The windows dark so I cannot see in. But I see the sign and I waver uncertain if this be the inn Margaret did speak of. True 'tis in Haven, of that I am sure. True this is an ale house. But I did hear Margaret call it 'The Pilgrim' and this sign shows pipers. I think, at first, there many of them pictured upon it, but then I see there be only one. The rest are children playing pipes and who are following him. Perhaps he is 'the pilgrim'.

As I stumble towards the door I do sigh out. For a cottage joins onto it. Just as she told me. This must be the right place. This is her house. Right next door. It will be her downfall I reckon. Too easy to sell the ale, drink the ale and then step next door to bed. With a customer for warmth if she desires. Or if they do and have coin.

I cannot complain, I think, as I descend the steps and go

through the heavy door. She has helped me in my darkest time and I will thank her.

But there is no one here. The parlour is bare.

No children.

No Margaret.

Only barrels. Pushed up on tables or fixed into the wall.

But my children should be here.

Where have they gone?

For a moment my heart hurts with a pain. Then a door opens and a young woman comes into the room. She exhales and her breath mists the air.

'Ohfuckinghell.' She speaks a language I do not understand. 'Heating's clapped out again.' She does not see me standing there but shivers, then wraps her arms around her and hurries over, head down, to the barrels.

I regard her with curiosity as she begins to move the cask. I have never heard such a racket as the gurgling that comes out of it. The girl takes large rivets in her nimble fingers, turns them and yawns. As she stretches I see she is wearing breeches. And a child's chemise that exposes the tops of her breasts. A foreigner indeed. Or else the world has turned upside down while I have been prisoned so long.

'Greetings,' I venture, in as clear a voice as I can. 'I am Margaret's sister, Avice.'

The girl does not hear me. I draw closer and rest beside a large vat that comes up to my chest. There are letters upon it with a strange patterning I have not seen before.

I try again. 'I am come to collect my dearlings? My babies – Christabel and Edmund.'

Again she does not hear me, or pretends not to. Instead she bends over and turns another toggle on the next barrel. Her breeches stretch and reveal undergarments beneath, thin like ribbons, with no warmth. And they call Margaret and me lewd! We would not perform like this one.

The thought angers me. As does her refusal to see me here, so now I raise my voice, 'Do you know where my children can be found?' This time I say it with such force that my breath ruffles the papers on the vat and one of them falls to the floor. The girl rounds quickly like a spinning wheel. Her eyes dart from side to side.

I raise my arm and wave to her. But still she does not see. Why does she not hearken to me?

She sees the letter, that is true. For she picks it up and puts it back atop the vat.

So I step out from behind it, and call, 'Hoi, hoi.' But she turns her back and returns to her barrel. And now I find within me a fury has begun to boil. Does she do this to keep me from my children? When I have walked barefoot through the snow for them? Yet I have been through worse, you see. Oh I have been through more than callous disregard and spite. One foreign peasant girl in thinning hosiery will not come between me and my childs.

'I asked you!' I say and move towards her.

Nothing. She does not even turn.

I draw myself up, and I breathe in the sharp air then I take her by the shoulder and with a stab of my hand, do quickly turn her round.

'Where are my children? Edmund and Christabel? Where are my babes?' I do bawl at her face.

And this time she does hear me.

For her face contorts: her eyes grow wide, lips pulling open, within them the tongue begins to loll. The girl gives up a bellow, loud and fierce, like a rutting bull.

The sound undoes me. I was not expecting that. And I step back and find myself screaming too.

For a moment, the girl gulps in and leans back against the barrel. 'What the fuck?' she whispers, her voice hoarse and dry. Her face has paled like that of the snow. Then she puts down her head and runs at a great speed across the cellar and out of the door.

And I think for a moment. Then I follow her out and find I am in in the road again with the hushed quiet and the frozen ground.

And I frown.

Where are my children?

Margaret told me she'd keep them.

I was sure it was here.

In Haven. Safe Haven.

She told me, she did.

Back in the prison.

Before they took me.

And then I try to place my remembering. Before they took me to . . . where?

And that hole threatens to engulf me again. That blackness in my mind.

And I try to resist.

But I cannot stop thinking on where they took me after she said . . .

But the rabbit hole draws me to it.

After Margaret took Christabel.

In the hole there is no longer nothing.

Christabel.

Bright sparks flit about like a blizzard, curling into a spiral around themselves.

In the hole there is a wind that pulls me in, sucking me down, whirling me. I cannot tell which way is which.

Above me the moon crosses the darkness, but so quickened now. The murky sky lightens. Clouds bubble and pitch in the gap. The sparks fade. I close my eyes and see inside my lids, fingers pointing, fingers pinching. And I hear a scream as I push Christabel out of me, and the arms take her, and the arms take me. And I step onto the gallows and I close my eyes and the blackness calls to me, and I step into it, falling, falling, and the darkness takes me. And I become it and it becomes me.

And for a moment there is nothing.

Warm, velvet nothingness.

And then . . .

And then . . .

Out. Free.

Into the light.

Into the night.

Barefoot in the snow.

Free.

It must be that the governor, no, not the governor – the

lord. Yes. I can only but think that the lord – not he in heaven – but he in the seat who judged me so – that the lord has felt his frozen heart thaw. Even in this midwinter bitterness.

What a time for it to be so.

But nothing surprises me any longer. The worst is come and gone . . .

A CHRISTMAS CAROLE

'Last night I dreamt I went to Mandelay again,' said Kieron and stowed the last dry pint pot underneath the counter. Over by the door, Sharon shepherded the final few customers out and locked up.

Carole sniffed. 'All right, all right.' She hated it when he brought this up. 'I told you I'd take everyone there for a slap-up, and I will. Just not now.'

'But it's Christmas Eve,' said Kieron. A pronounced pout settled on his lips. 'You said we'd go for our *Christmas do.*'

'Yes,' said Carole. 'But not while the prices are hoicked up so high. I don't know why people do that. I mean, we don't put up the prices in the pub. And we could.'

'It's just once a year,' sighed Kieron.

Carole pursed her lips. 'Old Faz has stuck a fiver on everything on the Mandelay menu. I don't know, I really don't. Seems to me it's just an excuse for picking people's pockets once a year and I ain't no muggins, am I.'

Sharon pressed her derriére against the front door to check it was firmly closed. 'No,' she called to her boss. 'That's not what we call you.'

The landlady, however, didn't wish to know what it was they did call her, though she had an idea. To head off a possible discussion she decided to astound them with generosity. 'All right then, who wants a drink?'

'That's very kind of you,' said Kieron instantly. 'I'll have a Jack D on the rocks.' It was, it had to be said, a highly unusual turn of events.

Sharon tossed a glance at Kieron and shrugged. Perhaps their tight-wad boss was turning a corner. 'Mine's a Baileys if you don't mind, Carole.' She waddled over and stuck her elbows on the counter.

Carole slid a tumbler full of whisky across the bar to Kieron.

'Seasons' greetings to you all.' He raised the glass with a grin.

Carole nodded, 'And you too, Kieron.' She glanced at the barmaid, who had an incredulous grin plastered across her face, and sent her a smaller shot glass full of the milky liqueur. 'Merry Christmas, Sharon.' Then a thought crossed her mind and she looked at her watch. 'Actually, it's ten minutes away, so Merry Christmas *Eve* to both of yous.'

'Either way,' said Kieron. 'Cheers,' and he took a large slug.

'That'll be three pounds eighty please,' said Carole.

The request made Kieron choke on his bourbon. 'You what?'

Carole shrugged. 'I've given you staff discount.'

'You're joking,' he spluttered, the whisky fast souring on his tongue.

Sharon mouthed 'Scrooge' at Kieron, heaved a sigh and threw four gold coins onto the countertop. 'Put the fifty pence change in the charity box,' she said and grabbed her bag. 'You never alter, do you?'

Kieron shook his head. 'She certainly don't.'

'I know – I'm no mug, am I?' said Carole and pocketed the silver coin.

Upstairs, half an hour later with the pub underneath locked up nice and tight, Carole kicked off her slippers and made to draw the blinds against the chill winter night. The wind was whipping up a fury out there. She could see the tops of the trees in the nearby graveyard shaking violently, as if dark unseen things had crawled from the bowels of the earth to shake the trunks and gnaw at their roots. She shivered and dismissed the thought as uncharacteristic fancy and went to sit on the heavily draped four-poster.

It wasn't her choice of bed, but it was so large and cumbersome it had been impossible to remove from the room. No one knew who the hulking bedstead had belonged to originally. Some speculated it might have been assembled when the pub was built sometime back in the sixteenth century. Personally, it gave Carole the creeps. If it wasn't technically the property of the brewery, she would have taken an axe to it many years ago. Or sold it. Probably the latter. But it was, and there was no way she was going to risk owing them money, not on your nelly. Not when you considered the pittance they paid her . . . No, she'd been caught out by landlords with inventories and deposits before so made sure that the big old bed was worm-free and regularly polished.

'More's the pity,' she said out loud and noted a crack in her voice. It was the cold air. At least she could draw the bed curtains around her and block out the drafts. That was the only bloody thing they were good for, she thought, and prepared to swing her knees onto the duvet.

A loud ring, however, stopped her.

It was an odd noise that sounded like a bell. And for a moment she froze and peered into the gloom of the bedroom. All was still and silent but for the shrill of the wind clawing at the window cracks. And for a second she wondered if she had imagined the noise when, tring tring, it came again. This time, though, she was able to locate the source and saw, with some relief, the screen of her phone glowing on the bedside cabinet.

Ah, good. She registered a little icon, shaped to resemble a bell, and the symbol of an envelope, which indicated someone had sent her a text. It was Christmas now, she thought. Possibly it was her son, Ben, sending her the seasons greetings. She humphed out loud reflecting proudly that she hadn't blessed him with her presence for a good while. Not since that business with the tunnels and the pickled knight. The feckless chancer was just like his long-lost dad and desperate to worm his way back into her fiercely protected heart. Most likely with a view to moving back in and sponging off her again. Like father like son, she snarled inwardly. But Carole was resolved against him and not having any of it. Ben needed to learn his lesson, man up and realise that if he was going to muck around then he had to deal with the consequences. He'd ended up with a mighty fine, and, secretly, she suspected he was after a loan to pay it off. But she would not do that. Not on your nelly. Carole Christmas was no mug.

She pressed the icon and the text unfolded. It wasn't from Ben. It was from Mandelay. 'Merry Christmas!' it read. 'You alone, out of many hundreds of our special customers, have been selected to enjoy a meal for two at Damebury's premiere restaurant. Congratulations. Call 01245 3666321 to book.' There was a photo of their menu underneath.

As she read the message she heard, in her head, the voice of Faz, the proprietor, and his erratic vocal emphasis, which betrayed the fact he was not a native speaker. Carole had an idea that if the offer was legit, she might perhaps be able to swap it up for a four-course dinner for one. She was very self-contained, not inclined to romance, which was reserved for fools and those who had money to throw away on other people. She fell into neither category, thank you very much. Nor wanted to. Other people just let you down or used you. There was no point investing in any one of 'em.

She read the message again. Perhaps she'd do it even if it wasn't kosher – she deserved a treat. It had been so busy lately. Kieron and Sharon would be none the wiser and if they did find out, then her reputation would hardly take a knock: Carole Christmas was known never to look a gift horse in the eye. Probably, though, it was just another one of Faz's off-the-wall money-making schemes that he was well known for. Like the 'free' Bombay potatoes that incurred a £4 'chopping charge'. Though most of the villagers took all his shenanigans with a pinch of salt, succumbing to the effusive charm of the bumbling restaurateur whilst acknowledging that his cuisine was probably the best in the county and good value for the price anyway. But it irked Carole, who liked to get her money's worth as much as the next man, as long as that next man proclaimed the thrifty ethos of a popular budget Irish airline.

Carole sighed and replaced her phone on the table. She'd get that dinner, one way or another. If she followed up the offer and was denied a free meal she might have a case with the Trading Standards. A phone call in their direction, or the *threat* of a phone call, might provide enough leverage to squeeze a free staff meal out of Faz. She'd think about it.

Extinguishing the lamp, comforted as always by the cheapness of darkness, she drew the bed-curtains close and pulled her duvet and blankets up to her chin.

No sooner had she shut her eyes, however, than her thoughts were interrupted by another ring of a bell. This was not electrical but distinctly metallic. A singular chime, she realised, must have resounded from the church across the road, travelling through the graveyard and into her room. Was it one o'clock? Perhaps it was. She nestled down into the bedclothes again and was almost about to slide into sleep when she heard something else: a movement on the landing outside her room. A dark sound. Heavy. Metallic again, but not like the bell. Oh no, this noise was more scattered and scratchy. Almost like chains, from the cellar below, were being dragged across the floorboards.

Carole bolted upright. Her imagination, which was not expansive nor taken to tricks, was playing up. Probably it was the effects of the undigested cheese she had snacked on before retiring. She poked her head out through the bed curtains.

The fog had poured through chinks in the windows so the room was full of dense mist. She must, she rued, get those panes seen to. But to what cost, she wondered? And who would pay. Not her, she hoped.

She was so taken with her lamentation over potential expense that it took a while for her mind to process what her eyes had settled on. But when it finally did, she jumped up and cried out, 'Oh my good gawd. Graham! What are you doing here?' For she could see the figure of her former colleague.

Graham Peacock had been an all right sort of bloke. Okay to work with. Easy, right up to the point where he'd had a massive heart attack and died.

Recollecting her colleague no longer walked the earth, Carole opened her mouth and began to wail.

'Oh, give up. You're making my head tingle,' said the late Graham Peacock. 'Do you remember me?'

Carole, shocked by the fact that the spectre could speak, complied and stopped howling, then squinted. Her eyes roamed over the silky patterned waistcoat and worn corduroys, which she realised were almost transparent. 'Course I remember you. Course I do. 'Cept you're deceased, mate.'

'Say that again?' Graham's scant eyebrows rose into his wavering head.

Carole smiled, pleased to see she had outwitted the apparition. 'I said, you're dead. Brown bread, dearly departed, pushing up daisies: DEAD.'

'No, before that,' said Graham, undeterred. 'You called me "mate". Oh good well, at least this might have an impact then.'

'We *were* friends of a sort,' Carole conceded. 'You were always kind. Before, you know, you carked it.'

Graham took a light step towards her. 'And I still am. You know, I have sat beside you invisible on many a day.'

'Ew,' Carole shuddered. 'What? Even in the shower?'

Graham shuddered back. 'No, not then. I still have my standards. I have been biding my time, waiting to find a good moment to talk you into counting your blessings and warn you about your future.'

'My future?' Carole smirked. 'Shouldn't you be worrying about your own?'

Graham shook his large see-through head. 'Ah, no. Mine's fine, thanks very much. Infinite and expanding. I was pleased although a little surprised to discover that I was quite a good egg, overall. No, it's yours we must pay attention to.'

'Mine?' It didn't make sense. Nothing did. And she realised she was obviously asleep. She must have dozed off before the bell and was dreaming now. Still, she might as well go along with it. If it got too bad she could try and wake herself up. 'Why do we need to think about my future then?' she asked Graham, going with the flow.

'Well might you ask,' replied her late colleague. 'I have been alerted to some news that, er, well, in simple terms there is, in fact, a special place in Hell reserved for you. Which is what made me pop down this evening and don the chains. Old fashioned, I know,' he said and rattled them. 'They still have a terribly dated idea of what ghosts are meant to look like. Anyway – we're allowed one manifestation a year, if we've been good boys and girls. Though it's hard not to be really. Not many distractions upstairs to lead you astray, if you know what I mean?'

Despite her self-assurance Graham's words were having an effect on Carole. Alarm was creeping into her fingertips and making them prickle. 'Did you say Hell? A place for me?'

'Y-es,' Graham nodded with deliberate slowness. 'You and several Conservative politicians, as it turns out. And I wouldn't wish Jacob Rees-Mogg on anyone. Not even the curmudgeonly Carole Christmas. And that's saying something. Thus the intervention.'

Carole blinked. She wasn't sure how to respond to that. I mean, you wouldn't really, would you?

'So,' Graham picked up again. 'It's pretty simple,' he said. 'You have to stop being such a cantankerous, mean-spirited, money-grabbing . . .' he paused. 'No, actually, I'm not meant to say that.' He coughed and cleared his transparent throat, a habit lingering from his earthbound incarnation. 'You're going to get a visit.'

Carole shook her head. 'I'm dreaming, aren't I? It's a dream sequence . . . I remember this . . .'

'No! Of course you're not dreaming. Why would you dream about me?'

'It's been a while,' she admitted. 'But I did think about you. For a bit. After you carked it. Thought you might have left me something in your will.'

'How very touching,' Graham muttered. Then he started, as if he had heard something, and cupped his hand to his ear. 'Ah, that's them calling me in now,' he said and made his hand into a trumpet over his mouth, so that his voice echoed. 'Come in Number Ninety-Nine, your time is up.' Then he laughed. It was a loose, rattling laugh that complemented, in a dark, menacing manner, the scratch of his chains on the floor as he walked clunkily backwards. With every step he took Carole noted the window raised itself a little, so that when the ghost reached it, it was wide open.

'Take heed, Carole,' he said thinly. 'Take heed for sure.'

And then he was nowhere.

A sharp gust of wind blew in the room and jolted the landlady to her senses. Carole realised she was shivering, and, feeling the claws of cold about her neck, she flew over and pulled the pane down with a crack. Peering into the darkness outside she saw the fog was thickening. In it she could see streams of mist were curling and uncurling, forming shapes. She blinked. For a moment they resembled long, extended restless phantasms with twisted faces, shaped to convey different expressions. Though all were hideous – warped with horror, misery and fear. She shrank back and closed her eyes but became aware of their noises: incoherent wails that conjured emotions of grief, guilt, sorrow and regret.

This was stupid.

Carole turned her back on the sight and galloped over to her bed, which she jumped into and quickly pulled the curtains shut.

For a moment she sat there, listening to her own short, shallow breaths, and became aware that, outside at least, the wails were no more.

Then a curtain fluttered.

Carole's heart filled with dread and, even though she could not really believe it was happening, part of her knew something was on its way.

First a skeletal finger, then a thin, bony hand crept into the tiny gap between the curtains.

'Nooo,' whispered Carole, and her heart started up again.

The hand continued to inch its way into her bed and up the drapes, which it suddenly tugged back. She wanted to close her eyes against the sight, but found herself paralysed, eyes wide, and saw there, as the curtains swept back, an unearthly creature standing by her bed. She was somewhat relieved that it was small and bore the semblance of a child. Though this was not any ordinary-looking infant. This creature's face was mean and grizzled and though it had the wrinkled appearance of an old man with long hair, it sat atop the undeveloped body of a five-year old. A skinny five-year-old at that.

Trying to master her shivers, Carole stuck her chin out defiantly. 'What do you want with me?' she cried, hearing her voice grate on her vocal chords. Fear had strung them tight.

But the creature didn't answer. It was dressed in a white

tunic with a sprig of holly in its free hand. With the other it released the curtain and then stretched its fingers out to Carole, indicating that she should take them.

Although she feared touching the creature, she was more afraid of what would happen if she did not comply, so did its bidding. As soon as her flesh met the little spectre's, it cooled to a Siberian chill.

The small unearthly creature led Carole over to the window and gestured for her to climb out. Carole shook her head.

'Come Carole,' said the creature in hushed tones. And as it spoke a lightness descended over her and she felt herself rise into the air. The two of them passed through the wall of the pub, into an inky blackness and then touched down into what appeared to be a playground. It was full of children and noise and sunshine.

'Do you remember it?' asked the spirit.

'Oh yes,' said Carole. 'I'd remember Greenriver Juniors anywhere. Look! The brook at the end of the field,' and a real and genuine smile relaxed her face. 'We used to play there in the summer. Wouldn't be allowed now – all that 'ealth and safety. But see, they've still got the geese there.' Where the concrete of the playground gave way to a grassy bank, a group of Brent geese were building nests. 'They used to come up all the time and sit there laying. Never thought nothing of it back then, but it was something wasn't it? The six of them there: Dancer, Prancer, Blixen . . . no . . . Were they the names or am I muddling it up with something else? I always mix them up. Them and the days of Christmas. What is it – five golden geese or something? Seven ladies dancing?

I don't know . . . who does? Do anyone really care . . .?' The spectre raised its bony hand and touched a finger to Carole's lips, interrupting her flow.

'What?' she said, looking into its strange, wizened face. Its eyes grew large and the finger came off her mouth and pointed over to the playground. Carole followed its direction and found a group of children playing ball in the corner. Beyond them she could see one little girl with blonde hair in a yellow dress. Sitting alone on a bench, she was watching the game.

'I remember her,' said Carole. 'Hannah Jenkinson. She had something wrong with her.'

'Regard the scene,' instructed the phantom.

They watched the girl on the bench break into a coughing fit. A few of the other children playing looked over, then shuffled off a few paces, further away.

'She died ten years ago,' said the phantom and put a cold hand on Carole's arm as they watched another little girl detach herself from the group. This one was scrawny and topped with scraggy dark hair. Visibly healthy, she ran over to the girl on the bench where she took out a yoyo from her pinafore and handed it to Hannah. Then very quickly the two little girls began to play.

'That's you,' said the spirit and Carole bent closer and squinted her eyes and saw that it was indeed her younger self. 'You still had generosity in your heart, despite your father.'

'He was a drunk,' Carole said. Her words were loaded with a familiar bitterness. 'Always thieving. Couldn't help himself.

Stole from Mum. Even took from my money box. Nothing was sacred.'

The two girls in the corner broke into a giggle as their yo-yos collided.

'Hannah never forgot your kindness,' the spectre went on. 'Called it a blessing – you spending time with her when others wouldn't. In fact, her first daughter was named after you, Carole.'

The landlady gasped in, surprised. 'A blessing? I don't bless no one.'

'And you don't count them either,' the phantom said. 'Only your coins.'

But Carole wasn't listening. She was holding out her hand to the little girl, meaning to draw closer. 'I don't remember. I . . .' As she moved, the playground shifted under her feet. Instead of growing colder and gravelled as she expected, she found it furry and tacky and looked down to see she was standing on a dirty carpet. In a pub. But this was not the one downstairs. This was somewhere far less salubrious. The ceilings were stained yellow with nicotine, the seats sticky and unwashed. A jukebox played in the background – country and western – mournful and long.

'There,' said the spectre and pointed to a man sitting in the corner on his own. He was staring at the table, nursing a pint. 'Look. It's Stephen. The one you mourned for so long.'

'Stephen Pope?' Carole squinted but could find no resemblance in the crumpled grey-haired old man whose face was red and livid like a lobster and whose hands clasped themselves over a protruding pot-belly.

'Well, I never. He was a smooth-talking ladies' man. Attractive, lean,' she told the apparition. 'Popular, I thought.'

'You were looking through the eyes of love. And no, he's not like that any more. He ran off with your heart, didn't he?'

Carole scoffed. 'Humph. Yeah, and Michelle from downstairs and the hard-earned savings I'd been putting away for a cot.'

'But Ben didn't mind sleeping in your bed, did he?' the apparition whispered. 'And in the end you two were happy.'

'No, he didn't mind the bed. He liked it,' Carole said, as the spectre waved her hand, wiping away the sad old man, revealing a small, unfolded sofa-bed where a baby and a woman lay.

They watched for a moment as a young Carole tickled her newborn son, who responded by kicking his chubby legs and chortling loudly.

'But where is Ben now?' the spectre asked.

Wind screamed round Carole's feet and the temperature instantly dropped.

They were peering through a window into a small bedsit. Three young men were standing to go. Carole could see one was her son. Despite herself, she smiled.

''Night then,' Ben said to his friends and opened the door. 'See you tomorrow?'

But the smaller lad shrugged. 'Got family stuff I'm afraid, mate.'

'What about you Stevie?' Ben asked, trying hard to disguise a plaintive note in his words. 'You free?'

The boy called Stevie shook his head. 'Sorry Ben. Not tomorrow. Same as Lee, I got family.'

'No, that's fine,' said Ben, and grinned brightly as he waved them goodbye. He took a breath and closed the door after them. When it had clicked shut he leant against it and sank to the floor with his head in his hands.

'What's the matter with him?' asked Carole and pressed her nose to the window, trying to catch the expression on the young man's face. 'Why is he sitting down there?'

'My time grows short,' she heard the apparition murmur.

'Oh God,' said Carole as the scene darkened. 'I know the score. I've seen *The Muppet Christmas Carol*.' She pushed her nose harder against the black pane but found she could not see within. In fact she could not see anything. 'I'm going to get another visitor like you. They're going to show me my future. And it's going to be grim and it's going to be bleak and I don't know if I'll be able to take it.'

'Ah, those were the good old days,' said the childish apparition. 'I'm afraid it don't work like that no more,' it said. 'Efficiency savings. We've been streamlined.'

'So it's just you? It's just this? My future – it hasn't started ...?'

But just then, she heard something that made her start. A tinny bell-like sound was coming from her bedside. Her phone again. She stopped speaking and grabbed it and stared hard at the screen. A message.

With trembling fingers she pressed the folder open.

It read. 'Alone, alone, alone.'

Underneath was visible a photograph of a neglected grave.

Carole moved her shaking fingers across the image and made it bigger so she could read the engraving on the tomb stone: 'Carole Christmas lies buried here. Un-mourned, unloved and alone.'

The shock of it made her react with such force she threw the phone across the room.

'It's not real,' she shrieked. 'I will not have it like that.' And she gave up a long, sustained scream, for she knew that truly it would be so.

'Mum!' another voice pierced her.

A head was protruding through the bed curtains.

What fresh horrors did the night have now to unfold? she thought and hid her eyes.

'Mum! What's the matter?'

The voice was familiar, she thought. And she opened her right eye just a fraction. It was enough to recognise the features on the head.

'Ben!' she cried. 'Ben! My son. Are you real? Are you really here?'

'Oh blimey Mum,' said the face, which she realised was now connected to a neck and a body and several other regular parts of the human composition. 'Were you on the spirits last night?'

Carole blinked at him, not so long since a baby, and touched his cheek as she used to, noting it was, thank God, warm and full of life. 'You could say that. What time is it? I haven't missed it have I? Is it still Christmas?'

Ben laughed, partly in confusion, but also at his mother's genuine affection. It seemed a very long time since she had been pleased to see him. 'No, you haven't missed it, Mum. But you are late. Kieron called me over. There was no sign of you downstairs and the pub's almost ready to open.'

'And it's Christmas Day?'

'That's right.'

'Then bless you, Ben. You and me we're going to have a slap-up meal. In fact, tell Kieron to stick a closed sign on the door. We're having ourselves a little staff party. On me. You deserve it. I ain't been the best of . . . whatever . . . but I'll make up for it now, my son.'

And Ben did as he was told.

And so did Kieron.

And Carole?

Well she was as good as her word that day and every Christmas after, of which there were many. Over time it became a saying in Damebury that of all the village it was Carole Christmas who knew how to keep the holiday. New friends believed she had taken the surname to mark the Yuletide festivities, as each year her generosity knew no bounds. Though she remained no stranger to Sainsbury's Basics brand for her own shopping (old habits die hard), she lavished both time and money on family and grandchildren. Indeed, it was fair to say from that year on, Carole Christmas blessed each and every one.

ACKNOWLEDGEMENTS

For Sean and Riley.

Big thanks to the ladies, all the ladies: Jenny Parrott, Thanhmai Bui-Van, Margot Weale, Harriet Wade, Juliet Mabey, Francine Brody and special agent Sandra Sawicka.

And to the gents: Novin Doostdar and Paul Nash.

Big cheesy thumbs up to Mum, Ernie, Dad, Pauline, Josie, Arron, Samuel, Arthur, William, Richard, Jesse, Kit and Obie, Joanne, Lee, Ronnie, Harry, Matty, John, Jess, Effie, Anais, Rye and Isla.

People who helped me with these stories are Xosé and Tatiana, Kate Bradley, Steph Roche, Sadie Hasler and Sarah Mayhew, Josie Moore, Sean Groth. And my gratitude also extends to superfan, the splendid Dr Twisselman, who told me what not to include!

Hello and thanks to all my lovely friends, too many to mention individually.

I also would like to acknowledge all my readers, especially the ones who get in touch on Twitter and Facebook. I struggled with Cornish names for my housekeeper and driver in 'She Saw Three Ships' until Rob Tripp and Heather

Henthorn came to the rescue with 'The Trevelyans' – so big thanks to you two. The housekeeper became Gertie, a suggestion put forward by the lovely Antonella Gramola Sands. And Merryn Trevelyan owes his name to Ellen Przybylska. So huge clap hands to all of you lot.

I really hope you enjoy the stories.